FORGING FREEDOM

Volume II

Freedom Forge Press, LLC
www.FreedomForgePress.com

Edited by
Val Muller

Forging Freedom
Volume II

Edited by Val Muller

Published by Freedom Forge Press, LLC

www.FreedomForgePress.com

Cover Design by Val Muller www.ValMuller.com

ISBN: 978-1940553054

In Loving Memory
of
Allen E. Egger, Jr.

Forging Freedom Volume II

Table of Contents

Publisher's Foreword

Eric Egger

I write this foreword in tribute to my father, who succumbed to complications from a long-term illness while this book was being edited. When I remember my father, I remember the love of freedom he instilled in me.

Children often realize later in life that they have become more like their parents than they ever expected; the qualities we once thought were "stupid" and "annoying" in our parents are ones that we embrace in adulthood. For all of the hopes and dreams we have, we come to realize that our parents were once our age, too. And they would have had aspirations of their own. At Freedom Forge Press, we share the belief that people should chart their own course in life as well as benefit from the rewards and consequences of success and failure. They should be free to pursue their own happiness without the artificial barriers that are often erected by government bureaucrats seeking to maximize their own power or reward a particularly well-organized or well-funded constituency.

Ever a hard worker, my father took advantage of the free society in which he was raised. He was the first in his family to complete a post-high school education, and he used the opportunity to secure a life-long position with a phone company. His knowledge of mechanics and engineering also led him to become a horologist in his spare time, fixing clocks and watches with the patience that became his trademark.

As a child, I benefitted from my father's love of freedom. I was one of those kids raised before the age of over-protection and hovering "helicopter parents." My parents gave me boundaries, of course, but within those boundaries I was given freedom. My non-supervised bike route took up many square miles, and despite a few falls and bad choices, I survived each exploration, learning and growing stronger from my choices. (For instance, I now know it is a bad idea to throw water balloons at the neighbor's dog!)

When Dad made his watch and clock deliveries, he let me come along, buying me my choice of newspaper or magazine from the local news agency in town. Dad took pride in my choice of *The Wall Street Journal*. Like Dad, I saw that this country offered great opportunities for entrepreneurs, and even though it took me the whole week to read a single day's paper, I did so. As I grew and understood the paper more completely, I saw the complications arising from government policies and decisions—and realized the world was not black-and-white. I realized that freedom is challenged daily by policies and motivations unknown to the general population.

Thanks to the foundation my parents provided, I pledged to remain educated and involved, watching out for our freedoms even when it would be more comfortable to remain blissfully ignorant. I joined the Army at seventeen (with my parents' permission) and founded Freedom Forge Press afterwards as a way to share stories of freedom to keep the flame alive.

Dad always embraced the spirit of individuals making informed choices. Like him, I believe that, given freedom and education, humans can use critical thinking skills to make choices that will better this world. Only too often, those choices are muddied by dishonesty and shrouded by back-room deals. My ongoing hope is for Freedom Forge Press to offer a place for extended dialogue that transcends the superficiality of 140-character tweets and two-second "likes" and "shares" encouraged by social media. Today more than ever, it is important to celebrate freedom and question the methods and motives that people in authority use to ask others to give up their freedoms in exchange for some temporary comfort or security offered by a government program managed by bureaucrats in a distant capital who have little connection to or understanding of the challenges people face every day simply trying to pursue their dreams.

A politician-turned-journalist recently quipped that rights don't exist in nature, they're granted by men and by collective agreement. But if this is true, then our "inalienable" rights to life, liberty, and happiness can most assuredly be alienated and taken away by popular vote, unpopular laws, controversial court decisions, and even executive decrees. Those are not rights, but mere privileges. And if we accept that we have only a government-granted privilege to live, be free, and pursue happiness, then we are surrendering the very spirit that makes us human.

In *Forging Freedom Volume II*, we asked people to share creative stories with a freedom theme. We received true stories and stories based on authors' ancestors and relatives each struggling for freedom. We received stories in which authors imagined dystopic ends to well-intentioned polices. Stories of individuals struggling to keep their flame of a dream alive despite the dampening effects of powers beyond their control. My father embraced the spirit of such individuals, and as the years pass, I find myself more and more like him—celebrating the spirit of the individual who succeeds in spite of the barriers that society and government erects.

Forging Freedom

THE SCHOOL

Melinda Friesen

Instructor Sigma walks the aisle between desks in our small classroom, scrutinizing our work. I curl up the corner of my worksheet to hide my sketch from her. I scratch my pencil over a scrap of paper to form a wide trunk, darting branches, and scalloped leaves like I've seen in books. Of course, no one has ever seen a real tree. No one with a pulse, anyway.

The floor trembles. I lift my head from my work and meet the other girls' questioning gazes. The desks jolt. The room shifts and shudders. The buzzing fluorescent lights flicker. Pencils drop off desks, and the stack of books on Instuctor's desk slides sideways. The portrait of our Leader rocks off its hook. Instructor lunges for the falling portrait and catches it before it hits the floor. The shaking stops, leaving only the sound of my heart thumping in my ears.

Instructor hangs the portrait. "Only a tremor. You know the earth is unstable. Return to your work."

No doors or windows allow us access to the outside. There's nothing to see out there anyway but scorched ground, animal carcasses, and charred remnants of trees. Trees. I've seen black and white pictures of them in books. I've read of their green foliage and of the blue sky and of the birds that used to sing and flutter through the air.

Instructor tells us we should be thankful. Millions died in the Destruction. The Leader saved us by creating The School, an island of Cinderblock walls floating in a sea of decay.

If I should be thankful, why aren't I? Why do I wish they would've left me in the darkness to die?

The Leader needs us to keep his machines running so he can harvest the mineral—the mineral he needs to restore the Earth. I try not to think too far ahead. Imagining my life spent beneath miles of dirt presses down on me, steals my breath, and twists my stomach into a knot.

Instructor paces, pointed shoes clicking, dark eyes gazing down her slender nose. Tufts of dust from the industrial tile floors gather on the hem of her soot-grey robe. The ring of keys dangling from her belt clangs in time with every rhythmic step. The silver key catches my eye. It's the key that locks us in the dark rooms on the lower level when we disobey.

Instructor's gaze falls on me. Her eyes narrow to empty slits. "What are you doing Cee-four?" I drop the corner of my mining machinery worksheet to cover my drawing and scrawl "manual pulley" on the diagram of a rock crusher.

Instructor stops beside my desk and eyes my paper before she slinks forward. I fold the scrap of paper—my secret tree—and tuck it into my bra before she rounds the last desk.

***

We file to the cafeteria for dinner. The Instructors place cups of lukewarm water and bowls of white meal in front of us. Bowls of nothing. No taste. No smell. Only a smooth, viscous texture like a mouthful of snot. It sours my stomach. The acidic tang of vomit would've been preferable; at least vomit has a flavour.

Jay-two stares down at her food, eyes as round as our plastic bowls. "Cee-four, that earthquake was stronger than the others." Jay-two sleeps in the bed below mine. She cries at night.

I stir my slop and nod.

Her shoulders hunch forward and she wraps her arms around her stomach. "What if next time it shakes the school apart?" Jay-two's voice trembles.

"Quiet!" Instructor Delta calls out.

I reach my hand under the table to find her cold, shivering fingers. I enclose her hand in mine and give it a reassuring squeeze. I glance over my shoulder to make sure Instructor isn't looking. "Everything is going to be okay. We're safe." I force conviction into my expression, though I don't believe my own words.

I lift the spoon to my mouth and drop the slurry onto my tongue.

They send us to bed after dinner. I'm never tired enough. I stare at the ceiling. Instructors patrol the halls. I wait on the top bunk for sleep, my only reprieve. In my dreams I see colours, trees, songbirds, and sometimes a woman's face. I press my palm to the Cinderblock wall. It's warm tonight. What's beyond that wall that makes it sometimes cold and sometimes warm? Isolation enwraps me despite the twenty other girls breathing in the room.

I conjure the image of the woman from my dreams. She always makes me feel safe. I can't decide whether she's a memory of something real or the memory of a dream. She has shiny black hair like mine and kind brown eyes. I've never understood her expression, but I think she was trying not to cry, trying to be brave. Her mouth moves. Sometime I hear her, "Jonquil, my Jonquil." She holds out her arms to me. I reach for her, but someone's pulling me away, further, further, and then she's gone.

Sliding my hand under the corner of the mattress, I retrieve my pile of paper trees and skim my thumb over their torn irregular edges. I line them up on my pillow and lay my head beside them. A graphite forest fills my vision. For a few moments I can feel something instead of greyness and warmth and silence. Footsteps stop outside our door. I gather my woodland and hide it beneath the mattress.

Before the morning alarm can scream its wake-up call, a bright ruby light pierces my eyelids. Beautiful blood red. I open my eyes and squint at the brilliant light oozing through a hairline crack in the mortar. I touch my fingers to the jagged opening. The light illuminates the tip of my finger. I've never seen something so bright. What is it? It can't be the outside. Can it?

The alarm erupts in its shrill keen. I arrange my pillow to cover the crack. I don't want the Instructors to know about it.

I struggle to concentrate in class. The light refuses to leave my mind. I doodle bricks and cracks and trees on the corner of my paper while we're supposed to be taking notes off the board. A hand slams down on my paper. Instructor's wrinkled, boney fingers cover my drawing, her veins bulging like boils in need of lancing. Her fingers bend at bulbous joints as she curls her hand into a fist, crumpling the paper. I wilt under her glower.

"Cee-four, we are taking notes."

I gnaw on my cheek. "I'm sorry."

"Recite the Guiding Wisdom."

The other students lift their gazes from their papers. Every eye settles on me. My cheeks warm until I'm sure they beam as bright as the light beyond the brick wall.

"All truth is experiential—" My voice cuts out. I clear my throat. "Nothing exists beyond what can be sensed."

"Correct. What, then, exists?" She lifts her chin and her cold

8

stare drives rusty nails into my soul.

I force air through my tight throat. "The Leader. The school. The Instructors. The students. The desks. Light." I feel myself crumpling into a mangled heap.

She smirks. "And trees? Are they truth?"

I wrap my arms around my stomach, not knowing how to answer. "Yes?"

"Have you ever seen a living tree? Touched a living tree?"

I shake my head.

"Speak up, so the class can hear you!"

The word claws its way out of my mouth. "No."

"If trees cannot be sensed, then what can we derive from that?"

I shift in my chair, drop my gaze to the faded and scuffed wood grain on my desk. I need trees to exist. I can't let her take them away from me. They exist in my mind.

"Cee-four! Answer me!"

I grind my teeth together.

She grabs my braid and yanks my head back. Her lips curl over yellowed teeth. "If they cannot be sensed, they do not exist!"

Hot tears flood my eyes, but I force them back. *Please don't put me in the dark room again.*

"You will spend the rest of your day on your bed." She grabs my arm and tows me up the stairs to the dormitories. I don't protest. I'm lucky I didn't get worse. I climb into my bed. She slams the door. Her footfalls grow faint down the hall. I move my pillow. The light has changed. It slithers through the crack from a different angle. I stare at its warm glow. It soothes my racing heart. I press my eye to the crack to try to see more, but it's too bright and leaves dark blobs on my vision.

I put my ear over the crack, the bricks heating my cheek. A whoosh and a wisp of air licks my ear. A whistle—long and lilting. High and low. My heart races. What's out there beyond the wall? Darkness and destruction as we've always been told? No. There's more. There has to be more. I need to see. We all got in here somehow. There has to be a way out.

I stuff my pillow under the blankets, climb down from the bunk, and creep to the door. Turning the knob, I ease it open and wince as it moans on its hinges. The deserted hall stretches before me, tiles reflecting the strip lighting. Murmurs of recitations hum beneath the floor. I slide through the gap in the door and close it again.

Pressed against the wall, I creep down the hall toward the janitor's closet. I've seen keys dangling from his belt loop. Keys to what? I don't know. I can only hope he has to leave these walls sometime and has a key to get himself out.

I throw myself into the janitor's closet and shut the door, letting out a heavy breath at making it this far unnoticed. I run my fingers over the wall beside the door in search of a switch. I flip it on. A dim single bulb flickers and flashes to life, washing the room in a putrid green hue.

I search hooks, shelves, breast pockets of soiled shirts slung over nails protruding from the wall. Nothing. A squeak in the hall penetrates the door. I lunge at the light, switch it off, and crouch behind a cluster of mops and brooms.

The door opens. I hold my breath. The janitor wheels his mop bucket into the tiny room, keys dangling from the back of his belt like a silver and gold chandelier.

My heart drums in my ears and I draw shallow breaths. If he finds me—if he tells Instructor—she'll lock me in the dark room again. After seeing the light, I can't bear the darkness anymore.

The janitor hums a slow tune, a discernable word breaking through between sandpaper notes. Age-spotted hands clutch the bucket. He groans as he crouches down, bringing his keys within reach.

He dumps the murky water into the floor drain. I stretch out a quaking hand, bite my lip as I flick the latch on the key ring and disconnect it from his belt. I yank my hand back and watch, afraid to flinch or breathe. Did he notice?

He stands up, refills his bucket, and rolls the yellow plastic tub back into the hall by the mop handle. The room falls black again.

I hold the keys to my chest and release a tremulous breath. In the darkness I form a mental map of all the locked doors I've ever seen. I can't go near the classrooms for risk of getting caught. Think. Think! How long do I have before Instructor will check on me and notice I'm gone? There's a locked door beyond the bedrooms, near the bathroom.

I pry open the door, peek out, and listen before dashing down the empty hall on the balls of my feet—past my bedroom, past the bathrooms. I slide keys into the lock, cringing as each key clanks against the metal. Five keys. Ten keys. On the eleventh, the bronze key slides in. I turn it and the lock clicks open.

Once inside, I lock the door again and dance my fingers over the wall in search of a switch, but find nothing. I step forward and my foot catches on something. I fall, thunk, against wooden stairs. I crawl up the stairs on hands and knees.

With no more stairs to climb, I wave my arms into the oily abyss in front of me before edging onto the floor at the top. I find a wall and stand up. Students' voices carry faintly through the floor. The smell of dust and mildewed paper tickles my nose. I search again for a light switch. I inch along the wall, making sure of each step before placing my foot.

Something brushes my hair and taps my shoulder. I clap my lips together to keep from screaming. I swipe my hand at the object. A string. I give it a tug and weak light struggles to reach the corners. Old boxes litter the room between stacks of grime-encrusted books.

Storage. I sneaked out and risked punishment to see a storage room?

I wander the vast room in search of another door, but the only way out is the way I came in. I drop down next to a stack of books and brush off the fine powdered dirt, scattering it in the air. No, not books—not like our books, anyway. They're flimsier with colourful paper covers. Smiling women and men pose on the covers. The date on the front of one reads, "July 11, 2018."

I flip through the pages and marvel at the trees, the people, the colours. They must've been from before the Disaster. A thin beam of light reflects off the glossy page. I look up. A bright glow seeps around the edges of the metal door penetrating the ceiling. I stack boxes until I can reach the slide lock.

I jimmy the lock open. My pulse races, and adrenaline tenses my body. I push my shoulder at the hatch and shove it open. Light flows over me. I close my eyes against the painful brightness. I jump and boost myself onto the platform, sling my leg over, and roll onto a rough, hot surface.

My eyes watering, I squint into the light and shade my eyes with my hand. It's more light than I've ever been exposed to. My surroundings slowly come into focus. I gasp. An azure sky stretches above me dotted with a few cotton-ball clouds. Warm air surrounds me and passes over me in cadenced gusts. It rubs my arms and lifts my hair.

A blinding light beams above me. The sun! It heats my skin, my flesh. Seems to reach down to my bones. I smile as if being introduced to a new person whom I just know will be my best friend. I suck in the fresh, sweet air. I breathe in so much that white spots sully my vision.

I stay low as I peer around. Chimneys sprout from long strips of black roofing. I crawl to the half wall at the edge of the building. I lift my head and gaze over the side. My mouth drops open.

I've seen grass and trees and lakes in black and white pictures in my textbooks, but nothing could've prepared me for this. The rush of colours and textures. And the smells! Fresh, sweet, incomparable to anything I've sensed before. I want to breathe in more than my lungs can hold. Everywhere, greens of every shade and leaves and slender blades of grasses and prickly pine needles.

A lake in the distance reflects the sky. Blue! So much blue. The water ripples as the breeze caresses it. Small lavender flowers punctuate deep green foliage. Bark, knobbly and pocked, in rich brown hues, wraps the tree trunks. A white-capped mountain on the horizon guards its kingdom. The marvellous trill of a bird—a real, live bird—floats on the whooshing breeze.

I've slept for fourteen years. Now I'm awake.

My head begins to spin. I grab onto the brick wall to keep from toppling over. They were wrong! The earth hasn't been destroyed. It's perfect. Beautiful!

The Instructors have been lying to us.

The Leader has lied to us.

I want to climb down the wall and run—through the tall grasses, between the trees.

But I can't leave Jay-two and the others here. I need to tell them! But, I can't move. I can't look away from the splendour. Anchored in place, I watch the sun dip low on the horizon. It paints the sky in reds, pinks, golds. The real sky. All this time it's been just beyond the brick wall. An entire universe!

I need to go before they discover I'm gone. I take one last look before I sink back into the hatch in the roof and plunge myself into the familiar darkness.

I sneak back to the janitor's closet. I wiggle the bronze key from the key ring and tuck it into my bra. About to drop the keys on the floor so it appears as if they fell off the janitor's belt, I pause, eyeing the silver key with the word "master" etched into its face. I free it from the ring and shove it into my bra with its sister. I lay the remainder of the keys near the floor drain.

Back in my room, I climb into my bunk.

Excitement sets me twitching as I wait for the other girls to settle in for the night and for Instructor to turn off the lights. Her footsteps retreat down the hall, growing fainter, then disappearing. I scramble down the ladder and kneel beside Jay-two's bed.

"Jay-two?" I whisper.

She rolls toward me. "What are you doing? You're going to get in trouble."

"I have to tell you what I saw. I snuck out this afternoon."

"Out?"

I nod. "Outside. Outside the school."

Her eyes widen. "How?"

"I took keys from the janitor. They've been lying to us. I saw the sun and grass and trees and the blue sky. I heard birds singing."

She gapes at me, brow furrowed. "The earth has been destroyed. It must've been a dream."

"No, it's real. Come with me. I'll show you." I grab hold of her arm.

She shrugs my hand away. "No, Cee-four. It's all burned."

"No, it's not. I saw it."

"You touched it?"

I bite my lip. "No, but I heard the birds. I smelled the flowers."

Jay-two shook her head. "That's not true."

"But, it is. Please. Just come with me and you'll see."

Tears gloss Jay-two's eyes. "Shh, stop saying that. They'll make us go in the dark rooms again."

The door squeaks and a gust of air brushes my cheek. "What are you doing out of bed?" Instructor's voice scrapes my ears. She marches across the room. I fall backward, look up at her.

"I. I. Had a bad dream."

She seizes my arm, digs her fingernails into my skin, and drags me to my feet. "And what does that have to do with Jay-two?"

"I just needed to talk to someone—"

"She's lying," Jay-two says.

I throw her a desperate glance. Don't tell. Please don't tell. Beds creak as other girls sit up on their mattresses.

"She said she saw trees," the girl in the next bed says.

"And blue sky," another adds.

Jay-two pulls her blankets to her chest, twists them in her fists. "She said she snuck out and she wants me to come with her."

Instructor Sigma grabs my face and squeezes. She moves her face close to mine. Her hot breath skims my nose. "Recite the Guiding Wisdom."

I swallow back the dust in my throat. "No!"

Instructor's lips curl over her teeth. "We don't tolerate liars here. Tell them all how you made up this story."

My voice trembles as I say, "It's not a lie. If you go outside, you'll see."

Her eyes narrow to a sliver. "This is your last chance. Recant."

I clasp my teeth together. Memories of the darkness of the lower floors tightens a cord around my neck. But, it's the truth. How can I leave all of them under these horrible flickering lights when there's a world of beauty beyond these walls?

"The sun is warm and bright! There's birds. I heard them singing! There are trees. They're tall and green. The sky is so blue!" I try to jerk my arm from her grip, but she holds fast.

"Liar!" She hauls me to the door.

"It's true. I saw it. It's true!"

I wrestle my arm away and bolt down the hall. Smacking into

a broad chest, I tumble backward. I jump to my feet. Someone tackles me from behind. A sharp pain cuts into my neck. A needle! I shove another Instructor off me. I spring up, but the room begins to whirl. I force my legs. Run. Run! I fall sideways, brace myself against the wall. My legs give out and I smack down onto the tile.

Three Instructors, faces flushed, hover over me. Hands reach toward me. I try to lift my arms to bat them away, but my arms weigh a thousand pounds.

The Instructors carry me downstairs. "Please no. Please no." Tears swell around the corners of my eyes and dribble down my temples. Instructor Sigma pries open a heavy steel door. The metal on metal grinding of the hinges echoes down the hall. The other Instructors dump me in the corner of the room and stalk back the way they came. The smell of stale urine poisons my nostrils. I pull in shallow breaths. Instructor Sigma towers over me. "You will stay here in the dark until you can tell the truth."

I open my mouth and force air through my throat. It takes all my strength to speak. "It is truth."

She cocks her head to the side and flashes a grin that exposes her crooked teeth. "I know. But, we can't have the others knowing, now can we?" She slams the door, the light fleeing the room with her. The deadbolt clanks into place.

My mind sketches the trees, swaying grasses, and blazing sun on the backs of my eyelids. Struggling against the drugs, I rest my head against the rough concrete wall—walls that I thought protected me from the destruction outside. All lies. My world is inside-out. The teachers, once my protectors, are now my guards. The School, once my refuge, is now my prison.

And the Leader? His plan for us. The reason I'm here. He'll take us from this dark place into another, so we can work on his machine.

He's not benevolent. He didn't choose me to save me! I don't have a word for what I am, but the idea is repugnant, an offense so deep my soul aches. I am his belonging. His possession.

They control me. They even took control of my body away from me. I concentrate on my fingers, force them to move. They flinch, then wriggle. I force my hand to move, the effort making sweat bead on my forehead. A series of spasms, then it obeys. My control is returning.

The image of the woman from my dreams flashes in my mind. I understand the look on her face now. Anger erupts, molten in my chest. She's my mother and they took me from her. My name is not Cee-four. My name is Jonquil.

The key I stole rubs rough and rigid against my breast. I try my arms. They're heavy, but I compel them, pushing until they budge. I have to get out of here. What awaits me beyond the boundaries of The School? I don't know, but I believe one thing more than I've ever believed anything else—uncertain freedom is better than the certainty here. And once I'm free, I have to find a way to free the others, to make them believe.

A new Guiding Knowledge germinates inside me, extending its roots and branches into every corner of my soul. What can be sensed is a lie. Truth is in the unseen. Trembling and weak, I reach into my bra, pull out the silver master key, and turn the warm toothy metal in my fingers. I go to discover the unseen.

Forging Freedom

TALLGRASS

Gerri Leen

I dream of grass blowing in the breeze—not this short green stuff that surrounds the houses in the fort, but tallgrass, covering the prairies. My pony would race through the grass—if he were still alive and not shot out from underneath me in that last raid. I had to ride behind Red Smoke just to get home.

But if I still had my pony, his legs would swim through the grass, and the grass would tickle my feet as I rode, as I led the People from the summer camp to the winter.

Buffalo would roam. The herds a thundering darkness sent by the Spirits of the Grandfathers for the People's use. The Grandfathers would have fought till the end, their war cries filling the ears of those who invaded their lands. Their ponies would have been dressed in warpaint, just as I dressed my pony the day he fell, his dun coat disappearing into the golden tallgrass, only the red and black of the paint showing where he lay.

I loved that pony. I gave Burning Feather's father five ponies to win her, but her father would have let me keep the five if he could have had my tallgrass-colored stallion. But I caught the pony in the way of the Grandfathers, and I would not give him up.

Should I have been as stubborn when it came to making peace with the white man? The Grandfathers would never have done so.

I know this and if I should forget, Red Smoke is happy to remind me of my bad decisions whenever he gets the chance. But I ignore him as much as I can. The Grandfathers are not here and I am.

"The colonel wants to see you." A small-eyed, white soldier stands in front of me. He shows me none of the respect I deserve as a war chief, but at least I see fear in his eyes.

"Tell the Colonel I am busy right now." I am not busy. There is, in fact, nothing for me to do in this camp and the soldier must know it. But he hurries off as if I was sharpening my lance for war and not just sitting in the sun getting fat.

Burning Feather comes over to me, her stomach large with a child that will never ride the tallgrass. If I had known she would carry my son or daughter after so long trying, would I have made the same decisions?

Or did she finally conceive because I gave up? It is a riddle I cannot solve. As if Coyote is laughing at me, the great bear of the prairies, who sits and does nothing and yet his seed is finally active.

She lays her head against my shoulder and sighs. She has never once berated me for my choices. She is a good woman, an even better wife. She wears deerskin even though the white man try to push their cloth on the women and children of the People. As if they know that change will come best through them.

I am proud of Burning Feather. I stroke her hair and whisper to her in the language of the People.

I have heard that the white man have tried to take the children of the People away in other forts that lie toward the rising sun. They forbid the use of any language but their own.

My child will speak as I speak. I surrendered but there are limits.

Burning Feather gets up and leaves me in peace. Red Smoke walks by but does not stop to talk. I am relieved. He often comes with big words of what should have been, words that he will never have to back up. He has been my friend since childhood, but he was never a man of importance, would never have had to face the decisions I did. He talked too much and accomplished little. Nothing has changed here in the fort.

A while later, I see the Colonel coming. He walks slowly, keeping in sight of me. It is a sign of respect: the open approach. A sign we are equals.

Even if we both know we are not.

"Tompkins said you were busy."

"As you can see." I gesture toward the as-yet untouched pipe that sits next to my worn buffalo cushion. The cushion is from the last big hunt, from a mighty bull that fought hard to live. Burning Feather stuffed its hide with tallgrass to make me a cushion worthy of a war chief.

During the two years I have been here, the cushion has grown flat with use. There is no tallgrass left to restuff it with, and I will not let her use straw.

Red Smoke, for all his criticisms, lets his woman use straw, and he said nothing when she traded his old buffalo robe for the white man's cloth.

"I have news," the Colonel says.

I wait, as is my way.

"The last of the war chiefs in this territory have made peace with the Great Father in Washington."

I feel a sadness that is only half strong. There is an inevitability to this moment. A passing of ways that I am only now understanding. "It is over," I say, and I don't mean just the war.

"It is over," the Colonel says, his voice solemn, but I think he does not understand me.

"The Great Father promised us a home always in view of the tallgrass." This was one of my demands. It had, at the time, seemed like the easiest of the demands. How could I not live near the tallgrass that grew everywhere?

How could the white man destroy something in such a short time, something that had endured for as long as the People rode the plains?

"You promised," I say again. I hate that I sound like a petulant child.

"That is proving difficult." The Colonel looks down. "I remember when I first came here, watching the grass blow and weave. It was like the ocean." The Colonel sighs and reaches into his jacket pocket, drawing out a packet of tobacco for my pipe. I take it with pleasure. The Colonel has the best smoke in the camp and he only shares with me.

"You are a good man. For a white man." I smile because I like this man probably more than I like Red Smoke. I think he would have made a good addition to the People. I am not making much of an addition to his people.

"You are a patient man." He does not add anything to that like I did. Does not say "For a red man." He watches his words: it is a talent few of his kind have in my experience.

"I wait. Sometimes that is all a man can do."

"Don't wait for us to keep our promises."

I stare up at him in surprise, see that he is watching some of the dark men, men who are the only ones in the fort who are disliked more than me and my people. The Colonel takes a deep breath. "Even freedom can be less than it seems."

He turns and walks away, and over him, I see a white owl like one in the tales of the winterlands, his snowy feathers gleaming as he wheels in the sky.

Then the owl is gone, and I blink hard.

Owls do not tend to fly in the daytime. No matter what color they are. And white owls do not fly here at all.

The last time I saw an owl, I was riding my pony, a deer slung over its withers, dinner for me and Burning Feather and those I would invite to share the feast. I ate and ate and stayed slim and powerful because the life of the People was one of movement. I know I should move more but find little will to do it. What use is slimness and power now? I do not hunt, I do not fight, I do not migrate from the summer to winter camp. I stay, lodged in this earth that is no longer my own and think useless thoughts.

I shift so I can pull the buffalo cushion out from under me and slit it open, pulling out a handful of the tallgrass. Lifting it to my face, I inhale deeply. But the grass is old—the smell is faint, and dust fills my nose. I open my fingers and let the grass blow off with the breeze.

"Grandson."

I look around, wondering who would call me that.

"Grandson."

The sound comes from above me, and I peer up and see a raven looking down at me.

I wait. The bird must surely have more to say than just that.

"One wish, my boy," the raven finally says. "I can grant one wish."

I have never felt close to Raven, but I am not about to miss this opportunity. "The way things were."

"I cannot move time."

I nod; this was a wish of a foolish man, drunk with dreams. "Then freedom for my people."

"You wish too big. Ask again."

"A home in view of the tallgrass."

"Too much again. Ask something else."

I am glad this bird was never my spirit animal: he promises everything and delivers nothing. "You are a trickster, Raven. There is nothing I can ask for that you will give me."

"You are wrong." The bird flies down and lands on my shoulder. He sits with surprising lightness, his feet barely touching as he clings to my robe.

"What should I ask you for, then?"

"The one thing I can give you. Hope." Raven pecks at my hair and pulls a strand free. "Someday, when you are long gone, things will be better."

"And now?" I rub my head gingerly. Raven may sit lightly, but his beak is rough.

"Now, I give you what tallgrass I can." The raven hops down to my cushion, which is whole again. The hide looks new, the cushion plump.

I lift it up and sniff. The smell of tallgrass fills my nose. The smell of the sun on the prairies.

The smell of freedom. Maybe the smell of hope. If I could think of what to hope for, now that everything has been lost.

Raven hops once, twice, then launches into the air. He flies high, alone in the sky, then he is not alone, is chasing a snowy owl. They both wheel and fly in front of the sun, silhouetted, white bird and dark looking the same.

Then they disappear.

I sit on my fat cushion that smells of everything I lost, load the Colonel's smoke into my pipe, and wait for something I will never see.

But maybe my child will.

Burying Sarah

Gillian Burdett

Sarah went to bed early, very early for her, nine o'clock, when normally she stayed up for the late news, and then Jimmy Fallon, at least through his monologue.

Cobber and Sarah had been watching Jimmy Fallon since he took over *The Tonight Show* nearly twenty years ago. It gave them comfort to watch it now. To see every night that part of the old world still continued on through all the upheavals of the past decade.

She had been tired all day, a vague feeling of unease had distracted her through dinner, and, after finishing the dishes, she went upstairs to lie down.

At midnight, Cobber turned off the TV and made his nightly round, turning off lights and locking doors. Back out in the living room he stood by the picture window, about to draw the curtains shut. A patrol car slowly drove past the house. His heart beat quickened. Paranoia, he knew, his reaction to the police, but he left the curtains open not wanting to look as if he had something to hide.

Upstairs in the bedroom he slipped off his robe. Something felt wrong, in the dark, something was missing. It was too quiet, the silence heavier than he ever remembered. He knelt beside the bed. Even before he placed his hand on Sarah's chest and found it still, he realized why the room was so quiet. It lacked the soft rhythm of Sarah's breath.

* * *

They both retired two years ago. Emily and Christian were both grown and moved away. For Cobber and Sarah life circled back. They lived as they did when they first married.

The bus tours were Sarah's idea. Day trips that started at dawn and returned them to town very early the following morning. They were inexpensive and fun. They were approved. Private vacations, a couple escaping off for a day or a weekend, while still legal, looked suspicious. What is it you can't do in front of everyone else?

Cobber and Sarah had been on day trips to Ellis Island, the Boston Spring Flower Show, and Mystic Seaport. They met Phyllis and John on a bus trip to Atlantic City. The Atlantic City trip was a whim. They weren't the flashy, casino types, but it was February, bitter cold and gray, depressing with the dirty snow and icy walks. Why not, for fifty bucks, step out of character for a day? That lark, going some place they never had any desire to visit, turned serious. It became a pivotal point for them. No longer were they dismayed citizens helpless to do anything but throw up their hands. What they learned on that trip empowered them.

Sarah and Phyllis paired off almost immediately. An unlikely match, Phyllis with her tapered red fingernails, red lips, blue dusted eyelids and orange hair twisted up into an extravagant beehive-type hairstyle. Phyllis spoke rapidly, her teeth going *click, click, click* like a trotting horse, sentence running into sentence leaping from one line of thought into another, then back again. Her hands, heavy with silver rings, arms heavy with bangles, rose and fell, turned and twisted, in front of her face as she spoke. Sarah's head bowed, nodded in agreement, but rarely did she get any words in between Phyl's. A small, amused smile on her lips, she told Cobber later that she truly did like Phyllis: "She has a good heart, you can see it there behind all her makeup."

They boarded the idling bus before dawn. Like the other passengers they were bundled in layers of sweaters and scarves. They welcomed the heat in the bus. Many brought bed pillows with them to resume their night's sleep on the five-hour drive to Atlantic City. Cobber took the window seat, he always did, preferring to study passing neighborhoods and landscapes to socializing on the bus. Sarah took her seat on the aisle and took out the crossword puzzle she had pulled from the morning *Times Union*.

"Is that this morning's puzzle?" The voice, high pitched and slightly nasal, came from across the aisle. Sarah lifted her head to answer, but Phyllis didn't wait for an answer. "I started it this morning—you know eight down . . . " She leaned over Sarah's paper, ran her finger down the list of clues. "There, Thespian, did you know that is an actor? I had to look it up. At first I thought it was a kind of monkey, so I wrote in chimp, but then I couldn't make anything else fit so I had to look it up—John, that's my husband . . . " She jerked a thumb towards the man beside her. "He says it's cheating to look up words for a crossword, but I don't think it is. I mean the whole point of doing these things is to learn more words, don't you think? That's what I use them for, so of course I have to look stuff up . . . I love these trips to Atlantic City. It's our fourth time . . . we went last year and made sixty bucks off a slot machine, but then I went and pumped all my tokens back into the same machine and lost it all—this year I'm going to be smart. Once I win, I'll move onto a different machine. That's how you get ahead. I've got a book of crosswords in my bag if you get stuck on that one and want to try another . . . I like doing the word search ones too, I got a book of them . . . " Five hours later, when the bus pulled into the unloading area behind Trump Plaza, Phyllis stopped to take a breath.

* * *

Cobber pulled a quilt up to Sarah's shoulders, tucking her in as he would a child. He wanted to keep her body warm for as long as he could, not yet ready to pull a sheet over her head. They had been married thirty-five years; his union with her had been his natural state for so long he couldn't begin yet to think of all he'd lost. He only knew what he would not give. Cobber pulled down a suitcase from the top shelf of the closet and began packing his clothes. He would have to call the children.

* * *

In a kinder age, Sarah would have been a tender mother, soothing her baby's whimpers with a calm mind, nursing her infant in the rocker by a sun-filled window, playing on the living room carpet with balls and blocks, rattles and dolls, just for the joy of it. Emily and Christian should have had a childhood of afternoons in the yard, gliding through the air on a swing, strolling down the sidewalk, waving to neighbors. But now the neighbors were hidden behind Stockade fences. Sarah was too nervous to let the children out into the yard for play.

Their children were born into a scared country, a country angry because it had to live scared. People preyed upon each other, fence gates that once swung open freely were padlocked, doors once left open to let in a breeze, a visitor, now slammed shut and were bolted. The neighborhood patrol, a constant watch, enforced the laws enacted to restore goodness. These laws tightened over the states like shrink wrap.

Emily, their first, a blonde, curly-headed girl with her mother's strong chin and bold stance, blazing eyes, and balled fists stuck into hers sides, ready to argue every point and was always on the side of justice. Christian, their baby, quiet and serious, watchful, not angry like his sister, but not accepting either. He observed, waited for the right moment to speak, then a slow smile spread and made him irresistible as a child, forgiven as a teenager, and missed as an adult when he left the country, not willing to fight for ideals he never knew.

Emily wouldn't give up. She fought—high school debate teams, law school, the crusade— "It's a matter of dignity," she explained, loading the trunk of her car with books and clothes, slamming the hatch shut. She moved to the nation's capital, into the festering middle of it, believing her words were a lance that could pierce the boil. Christian never knew what his country had been, or understood what it could be. By the time he was old enough to look, he could only see what his country had become. He chose Canada.

"We did our job too well." This Sarah said the August morning they stood in the drive and watched Christian drive off to college. They knew he wouldn't come back. Emily and Christian both—independent, individual, they flew off, Emily to save her country and Christian to make his life in a different one.

Christian wrote songs in his Montreal apartment; he cooked in a Greek restaurant for money. Canada took the Americans in with no questions. Christian tried to convince Cobber and Sarah to cross the border. He could make room for them. They said no, not ready to give up, but it was a standing offer.

* * *

The casinos made Sarah giddy. She'd never seen anything so wild. Mobs of people poured from the buses and descended on hundreds of slot machines. Everything ornate, garish; polished brass railings, mirrored ceilings, red carpets, sequined cocktail waitresses. The flashing lights and ringing bells were overwhelming. She stood beside Cobber and squeezed his hand, saying, "This is all so silly!" But her face lit up under the crystal chandeliers. There is room for silliness here.

Phyllis dragged Sarah to the slot machines; the men, amused, leaned back to watch. Easily, Sarah went through a bucket of tokens. She shook her head and laughed, looking over at Phyllis mechanically feeding her own slot.

"We've been here all of five minutes and I've already blown ten bucks! To think I clip coupons to save thirty-five cents on a box of cereal. It's crazy; money doesn't mean what it does back home."

Phyllis smiled, breaking for a moment the concentration she had fixed on the machine's spinning dials.

"That's the fun of it, a new world with new meanings."

She resumed her motions, feeding in tokens, pulling down the lever.

"I just keep doing this until my arm falls off."

Sarah smiled at the image.

"Well, I'm sure Organ Distribution will be by to pick it up for you."

Sarah's joke soured the instant it hit the air. Phyl's arm, about to slide in another token, stopped mid-air. John raised his eyes from the patch of carpet he'd been studying; Cobber stiffened.

Later, with the four of them seated around a cocktail table in one corner of the lounge, John drew a map. He didn't label it, just drew blue lines with a ballpoint pen on a paper napkin.

"It's our way of fighting," he said, pushing the napkin to the center of the table. Cobber picked it up, folded it in half, and slipped it into his jacket pocket.

* * *

The blood donor laws were the first to pass. Cobber and Sarah used to donate regularly, every time the blood mobile came to the high school gym, freely giving life they had an abundance to give. Cobber's old driver's license was tossed in the junk drawer with old batteries and shoe strings. The box on the back was checked off—*ANATOMICAL GIFT TO BE EFFECTIVE UPON MY DEATH*. The new licenses didn't need this option; it was no longer a choice.

They watched the debates on C-SPAN although it wasn't much of a fight—the small opposition was too liberal or maybe too conservative. No one knew the definitions by that time. The debate never got beyond name calling and wretched stories about children dying in hospital beds.

Sarah was nine months pregnant with Christian then, her body so filled with that child it became her identity. She smiled each time he turned inside. She told Cobber that even in her sleep she was aware of the baby there and held her belly so as to hold her child. The baby reached all parts of her. She was filled with fluids and smiled quietly to herself and the rolling, like waves, inside her.

It was summertime, warm, but Sarah put on a sweater. Out in the driveway she squatted behind her car, rocking, off balance at first by her over-sized stomach. With a razor she scraped off the bumper sticker—*Blood donors make better lovers*. It had been on there for several years and would only come off in shredded bits. It took her twenty minutes to completely clean it from the chrome. It tired her, balancing her swollen body on the driveway gravel. "It's not love when it's forced on you," she said. "When it's forced, it's rape." Bone marrow came next, no debates. Who would vote against children with Leukemia?

The organ donor laws were argued in court. Oddly enough it was religious groups that led the protests; a brand of Christians that believed a body had to be buried intact to wait for the resurrection.

Sarah and Cobber weren't worried that their picked-over bodies would miss out on the after-life. They opposed for another reason, a reason they couldn't put words to. The laws, it seemed to them, violated something very basic, something very American that ran deeper than a flag or a national anthem.

They attended a rally, not to add their voices to the crowd but to listen, and watch, to see they weren't the only ones. It was mostly the Christians, but Cobber thought this issue must be confusing for them. Didn't Jesus give *his* body? On the edge of the crowd a young woman stood quietly holding a hand lettered sign, *"THE SOUL OF THE FLESH IS IN THE BLOOD."* Only a year ago Cobber would have labeled that woman as a religious fanatic, but somehow, now, she seemed to be the sanest person there.

Names of potential donors were compiled from voter registration lists and motor vehicle records. It was luck of the draw. Sarah gave so much. It was years ago, their children still babies, but the scar never completely faded. They had tried to fight it, claiming hardship, young children at home, the youngest still nursing, but some man in Connecticut needed a kidney. The judge had no sympathy for Sarah's pleas to be given a waiver, at least until her baby was weaned. That was Sarah's greatest concern, being away from her baby, even if only for a week.

She expressed milk and froze it, hoping that would keep Christian until she returned, but her hospital stay lasted two weeks and in that time, her milk dried. That, to her, was the greater loss. She didn't miss the kidney.

* * *

They went north in early October, a fall foliage trip to the Adirondacks for antiquing and a little golf. No one would suspect them. They filed their itinerary with the Neighborhood Patrol, acting casual; *we need a little change of scenery, fresh mountain air.* No one would know their true destination, the map drawn with a blue ballpoint pen on a tissue thin cocktail napkin. The X marked the grave yard they sought, a plot under the forest canopy.

They booked a room at a Bed and Breakfast and left on a Friday evening. "We want to wake up in the mountains," Cobber said. The watchman slapped him on the back. "Have a great time." He had a hearty voice. "And don't worry about a thing. We'll keep a sharp eye on your place while you're gone." No different than when I am here, Cobber thought but wouldn't say out loud.

Chenille bedspreads, lace curtains, and hardwood floor. They did this often when they were younger, before the kids, country inns, out of the way places. They'd forgo the free breakfast and lay in bed all morning, planning the future, dreaming of it.

Sarah had chestnut hair, and it was still thick as it always had been. Looking at it spread across the pillow, Cobber forgot, for a moment, why they came. It felt like a vacation, back in a freer time, filled with that sense of openness that came with unplanned time, unwound living. They could go where they wanted, blue skies and scarlet trees, brisk air, a pumpkin stand across the street, Indian corn and fall flowers. Sarah woke, smiled and stretched, sunlight flooded their room. "What a gorgeous day."

Cobber nodded. "Good day to be breaking the law."

The trailer appeared just as John said it would, a rusting cylinder of metal set into the woods. Maple saplings sprung up from its skirting, and low pine boughs masked its windows. Rotted wooden steps tilted to one side, coming several inches short of the screen door hanging by one hinge.

Cobber turned off the ignition, and in the hush that followed they sat in the car staring forward, waiting for something, not sure what.

"This must be the place."

Sarah nodded and chewed her lip.

"Do you think this guy went out of business? I can't believe anyone really lives here."

As she finished speaking, the trailer door swung open and a gaunt figure materialized in its frame.

The grave-tender was a tall bearded man, perhaps a logger, or once a logger, now a hermit, for whatever reason, holed up on the side of a mountain. Cobber knew his usual, cheerful greeting, extended hand, would be out of place there in the silent wood. He opened the car door and stepped out. Sarah followed and together they approached the trailer.

"How can I help you folks?" he asked, his voice surprisingly tender. Cobber and Sarah stopped their approach.

"John Krauss recommended you."

"I don't use names up here."

The man came down the crooked steps and stepped to the ground as quietly as if he'd been wearing moccasins. "Follow me."

Several logging roads branched off from the header where they stood. He lead them up one. "Remember this trail," he told them. "I might not be here when you need it."

Cobber nodded and took Sarah's arm. The woods changed gradually as they walked from the colorful, sunlit hardwoods into the deep, musty pine and moss. Birdsong faded behind them, and the autumn seemed just turning towards winter. The air hung heavy with cool moisture, a prelude to snowfall that soon would come. Then, at once, they came to the graveyard. That is all it could have been. Deep trenches dug at jutting angles, mounds of dirt piled by each. Sarah gasped, and Cobber too felt unsettled at the sight of the forest torn up so unnaturally. It looked like war's aftermath, or the scene of a police investigation, excavating for bodies, but this was in reverse. The holes did not hide death but instead stood open, waiting to swallow the bones, cover up the evidence of life.

The man stopped and turned at Sarah's gasp, raised his eyebrows in question.

"It's not what I was expecting," she explained. "Why are the holes already dug?"

"Frost is coming; I have to do it now." It made sense, that what they had come to expect in their lives no longer could be. He had to dig before the ground froze, having only a shovel to work with. No backhoe could work through the trees and even if there were room, a backhoe in the woods would draw attention. And the graves, not lined up neatly like a church yard cemetery, of course not. He had to work around the roots.

They paid for one plot. It was all they could use. No one would be left to bury the survivor.

* * *

Cobber brought his packed suitcase to the garage and lay it on the floor of the back seat. He threw his bag of golf clubs on top for cover. He returned to the house and began to look for whatever else he should take. The photograph albums, they were important, and the scrapbooks Sarah kept, one for each child, she would want him to take those. What else to take? He didn't know. Over the years, they collected many nice things, but now the meaning had seeped from them. In the kitchen, held to the refrigerator with a magnet, was a note Sarah wrote him the day before:

> *Cob,*
> *Gone to the store to find something for supper. Pete came over to borrow our post-hold digger. I couldn't find it (the garage is a mess!) Could you find it and run it over to him? Be back soon. Love, S*

Cobber pulled the note from the fridge and slipped it into his shirt pocket. He went back upstairs, rolled Sarah's body up in the quilt, and carried it down to the garage.

He didn't need the map this time. He found the woods and carried her body through them like a groom carrying his bride. He found their plot, laid her down on a bed of moss, then fell to his knees. The earth smelled good this deep in the woods. Fertile, rich, moist pine and winter green. He raked his fingers along the forest floor until his finger tips hit on the plywood that covered her grave.

He knew it wasn't Sarah there beneath the dirt at his feet, but the body he once held, loved, the body that held her presence on the earth. It deserved some words, but he could think of none. It was pointless, dropping her into a dark hole, even as a statement; this statement made in darkness would remain in darkness. Somewhere in Connecticut Sarah's kidney lived on. Like a garter-belted centerfold model, healthy and pink and drained of any soul.

He drove out the way he drove in, crawling over the dirt road aided only by moonlight. Once back on the main road, he switched on his headlights and pointed his car towards the Northway. By his watch it was three a.m. He would make Montreal by dawn.

It Won't Be For Long

Jordan Legg

"Are you ready?"

"I am."

The opening of metal hinges echoed in Hugh's ears, and he heard the sound of heavy footfalls in the passage outside. A set of keys jingled in someone's hands. The old man gripped his crutch tightly and looked up to see the door swing open. A large jailer stood in the doorway before them, wrinkling his nose at the excremental stench. He surveyed the two men and then stepped into the cell to gather up the aged Hugh in his massive arms. After flinging the old man over his shoulder, the jailer gave John a kick.

"Up," he growled.

John's hands groped at the floor beneath him until they finally hit the stone wall. The jailer carried Hugh out of the cell, and John felt a shove in the back directing him to move forward. Their officers took them up the stairs of the dungeon and eventually into the open air. Hugh's feeble body was flung roughly onto the back of a waiting horsecart, and John, too, was lifted up and placed beside his comrade.

"To Stratford-le-Bow," the jailer told the cart driver. The driver whipped up the reins, the horse gave a whinny, and the wheels of the cart began to bounce their cargo up and down over the cobblestone streets of London. The cart was flanked by two black-clad men-at-arms astride large black horses, baring their weapons to ensure an orderly execution.

Hugh put his crutch aside and tried to turn to better see his companion. The crutch had not helped him walk in years, but he had always carried it with him out of stubbornness. He winced as his hands forced two limp legs around, cursing the paralysis that had plagued him for over four laborious decades. A little grunt escaped his throat. He ground his teeth together.

He had not always been lame. As a child his legs were weak, but with the right effort, they had been able to carry him about his father's house. But as he had grown older, they had begun to grow frailer, flabby, as if their bones might any moment bend like grass. The first time he collapsed he had been standing on a ladder, helping his father paint a neighbour's barn. He had crumpled to the ground, and after coming to, he saw his father standing over him, cradling his head and asking him questions. He tried to stand, but after a few small steps, he keeled over a second time. He remembered with dread the few moments in which he waited on uncertain legs, desperately trying to muster the strength to stand, and then despairing as his body fell slowly, miserably toward the ground below. Two days later, his father fashioned him a crude set of crutches out of tree branches.

As the years passed, his legs had grown weaker and weaker, and eventually he had ceased to walk altogether. He had spent a few years at his father's trade of painting, but as his father grew older, the trade grew poorer. When finally the old man died, Hugh was left with no recourse but to compensate for his disability by the mercies of others.

He sought the pity of the Church, which his father had extolled with his dying breath. Hugh had been dutiful—he had prayed and fasted, and dragged himself into Mass with the pious hope that he might find favour in the eyes of God. He had heard the priests tell of the healing that awaited the faithful, and seen them parade their indulgences through town with the promise that when coins in coffers ring, souls from Purgatory spring.

But he had no coin for an indulgence. He could not buy the blessing of a priest. And not once had he tasted the blood of Christ at the Eucharist—it was reserved for clerics only, lest the commoner spill a drop and tread upon the blood of God. If he could buy no indulgence, nor partake in the holy wine, what hope was there for the salvation of his soul?

It was then that he heard rumours of men like Christopher Lyster and John Mace. Lutherans, it was said, who preached that no indulgence would save men from the fires of Hell, but rather by a free, naked faith in Christ and in his death and resurrection. No prelate was needed for this sacred faith, Hugh heard—only the plain Scriptures, which had now been translated into the common English tongue.

He had sought out Lyster and Mace, and had thus met the young John Apprice, who sat before him now. Hugh had known what his allegiance to these Lutherans meant—it was a heresy punishable by death. They had all plainly told him so. They had known this was coming. Their entire fellowship had been telling one another to be ready for the stake long before any had been arrested. In this company, with these books, and in this Eucharist there lies danger, they had told one another. Every man and woman among them had known it. And now their fears had come to fruition. Hugh and John had been preparing for this ride ever since casting their lot in with the Protestants. And not two weeks ago, they had been discovered by Bishop Bonner's men-at-arms. They had been seized and tried, and then there in Newgate they had waited for their sentence to be carried out, hoping and praying that when the time came, they would be given due courage.

He remembered the meetings that they had had together, he and John Apprice and the others that had met to break bread in secret. They had met in houses, secretly, praying and worshipping together. Someone had brought in Tyndale's New Testament, and together they had marvelled at the words they found in that forbidden text. Now, here, riding down this old cobblestone street, caught at last, Hugh reflected on the death that would surely come.

He had not expected it to be like this. All the hours spent in introspection, in steeling his spiritual grit for his inevitable final hour, seemed wasted upon knowing that the hour had come. This day, Hugh Laverock and John Apprice would stand before God. All he had yet hoped for in his earthly life was cut short. They would see no earthly retribution, he thought. He would not see the fate of the rest of their little Protestant congregation that yet waited, some in Newgate Prison, and some still at large and safe from the wrath of Bishop Bonner. There was this day only, and then he would behold Christ, waiting for them on the other side.

"Hugh," John said.

"Aye, John."

"Are you afraid?"

"No," the old cripple told him with a grimace, and in that moment, wondered if he had told the truth. "We'll burn today, John— that much is certain." He wished his voice did not tremble so. "But I know wherein my hope lies. And before this day is out," he forced a smile, "I shall walk again."

"I'm afraid, Hugh," whispered the blind man. "It is my last day without my eyes. Tell me what you see."

Hugh looked about him. "The whole of London's waiting round

us," he said, "with folk of all sorts watching us and walking alongside the cart to the Stratford stake." His voice grew strained and heavy. "There's scorn in some eyes and sorrow in others, and in some it's hard to tell between the two. Bishop Bonner stands beside the waiting stake, arrayed in rich prelate red, and round him his men-at-arms pile bundles of kindling round the faggot. They're readying it to be lit."

John nodded. "What else?"

Hugh found it hard to describe anything more. His eyesight was not what it once had been, but even in his old age he found it hard to imagine a life of total blindness. How could he describe what else he saw?

"Just speak, Hugh, please," came the plea from the man beside him.

"He's flanked by other clerics, doctors and priests in their black robes," said the old man. "A few knights on horses lie on the outside, watching to make certain there be no mischief here. There are drummers standing round the stake in a circle, waiting for their orders. The old stone chapel lies silently yonder, as if watching and waiting for when they set the flames."

"See you any of our number?" John asked nervously.

"Aye," Hugh whispered, his voice shaking. "A few, here and there."

The cart stopped before the waiting bishop, and a few men-at-arms dragged Hugh off the cart and up onto the platform, where the waiting stake stood like a bone, waiting to be clothed in the flesh of its victims. Hugh grabbed hold of his crutch as his handlers shoved his body up against the piece of wood, behind the stack of kindling, and chained him under the arms to the pole. One of them moved to take the crutch from him, but the paralytic dropped it before he could take it away. He hung there, limp and trembling. Yes, afraid.

The proud bishop stared down at the old beggar, and raised a scrutinizing eyebrow. His mouth pursed with haughty self-righteousness. Hugh thought back to the trial, six days before, when the bishop had demanded the two men confess transubstantiation, and when he had insisted that only through the Romanist sacrament of body and blood might one receive the mercy of God.

The men-at-arms thrust John down against the stake on the other side of his companion, and together they began to tie his arms around it to secure their victim.

"Tell me more of what you see, Hugh," John whispered to him.

"It's a bright blue sky over us this morning," Hugh told him, "with the sun shining down upon trees greener than I've ever seen in all my days. It makes me wonder what they'll look like in July, when all the world is in full bloom."

From the other side of the stake, Hugh could hear the blind man emit a nearly inaudible whisper. "Today, Hugh," he said with wonder, "today at last I'll see it."

"That you will," replied Hugh. He ran his hands around the unfeeling legs beneath him, crumpled between the kindling and the stake. For a moment he felt the weight of despair—what if their reward did not come?

What if the grace of Christ did not wait for them on the other side of death? What if they were to be met, not with resurrection in the presence of God, but the agonies of Purgatory, or worse, the fires of Hell itself? Or what if there was nothing at all beyond the stake? A terrible, aching emptiness, a non-existence, a cruel trick by a world indifferent to pain and injustice?

And yet it was so tempting to imagine the vigour rippling through his muscles. Standing up straight for the first time in forty years. He yearned for the sensation of strength in those old bones—the glory of standing tall the way men were meant to do. How long it had been since that strength had been his—and today, at last, it would be again. He thought back to his childhood, and the feeling of bare feet against the cobbled streets of Barking Parish.

"And I shall walk, John. Finally, I'll know what it means to walk again." Even as he said it, his voice began to grow more excited, and quickly he whispered, "It won't be for long, John. It won't be for long—and then at last you will see. We will see. We'll see him."

The drums began to roll, and the crowd grew quiet. Faster and faster the drummers pounded their sticks against the skins, echoing Hugh's pounding heart, and finally, they stopped. Bishop Bonner spoke.

"On this, the Fifteenth of May, in the Year of Our Lord 1556, I find Hugh Laverock and John Apprice guilty of heresy against the traditions and doctrines of the Roman Catholic Church; namely, the rejection of the Eucharist, of the veneration of the saints, and of the preaching of indulgences and Purgatory. Yet even now, God's mercy is at hand, if only these two men will humble themselves and recant their blasphemy against the Church of God."

Hugh thought for a moment of the fire that would come if they persisted in silence. The terrible consumption of flame over their flesh. His tongue trembled. It wished to succumb to the bishop's taunt. But no sound came from his mouth. He wondered if he was too afraid to speak up, and prayed for the reprieve from the temptation to speak that came with silence.

"Very well. Hugh Laverock and John Apprice, guilty of heresy, are hereby sentenced to be burned at the stake. May God have mercy on your souls."

The men-at-arms lit the torches and thrust them into the kindling beneath the two men. The stifling smoke climbed through the kindling and filled their noses. Heat began to intensify against their skin. The bishop glared at them with cold arrogance. Hugh could see the beginnings of a blaze growing beneath the shade of the kindling around them. The flame shot up, and the sound of crackling filled their ears. John panted frantically as the heat rose quickly around him, like a dog leaping up to grab fresh meat dangling just above its reach. A pitiable, suppressed whine leaked through John's tortured lungs, and his eyes widened, darting frantically across the platform, as if they might find some way of escape.

"Hugh!" he cried out.

Hugh bent his head back in an effort to behold his companion. Fear was audible in John's desperate breaths, and visible on his tormented face.

"Be of good comfort, my brother; for my Lord of London is our good physician." The crippled man inhaled deeply, but could not contain his breath for very long. "Oh," he sighed, "oh, he will heal us both shortly." He took a laboured breath. "You of your blindness, and me . . . me of my lameness." Pain seared through him like he had never known before, and he heard a tortured scream erupt across the square. It was his own. "Hold on, John," he cried, "it won't be for long." He gasped a lungful of air. "Remember the text: 'These are they which came out of great tribulation—'" He gave another wild, painful scream. "'—and have . . . have washed their robes and made them . . . made them white, white with the blood—" He cringed with the sting. "—of the Lamb.'" Out of the corner of his eye, Hugh saw the tormented head of John Apprice nod violently, banging against the stake.

The flames ran madly across the cone of kindling round the stake, and he felt the scalding heat against his own leathery skin. The flames licked corrosion across him. His breath vibrated loudly back and forth across his throat as he fought the fire for the air around him. It was like a ravenous animal, consuming, suffocating its condemned victims. Smoke, dry and unfeeling, filled his nostrils. It grew harder to breathe; harder to concentrate. He winced, and his teeth churned against one another. He could taste blood on his tongue as fire charred his trembling flesh. Hugh hardly knew what to hope for as he felt the fire deepen its scars across his ancient body. He had often wondered whether death would be painful—and perhaps for others it was not. But he could feel it all—every terrible, excruciating cut. He reminded himself silently with each passing minute—it's that much closer. That much closer to the end. That much of it is over with, and afterwards—

No. Not an end, he knew. A beginning. He would walk again. Today. He knew it, as surely as he had known anything. And surely that was not his greatest reward. Today, he thought—today he would see beyond that global veil. Today he would look upon Christ, and run, laughing, into his waiting arms. Today he would hear, "Well done, good and faithful servant." He just needed to hold on. It wouldn't be for long.

Author's Note: *Hugh Laverock and John Apprice have been memorialized in a monument to eighteen Protestant martyrs burned at the stake on various days in AD 1556 in Saint John's Anglican Church in Stratford, London. Their story is taken from the inscription on that monument, and their entry in Foxe's Book of Martyrs. This story was previously published at* Circa Journal *Issue 1.2*

Birth of a Rebel

Dixiane Hallaj

Boom! Boom! Boom! The steady beat of the drum echoed across the valley. Nadeem's hand stopped in midair, and his heart started thudding like a faster echo of the big drum.

"Do you hear it, Nadeem? They've come." The rustling of the thick foliage overhead accompanied his brother's voice. "Come on, let's go." Soon a bare foot poked through the broad leaves of the huge fig tree, followed by Amer. He wiped his sleeve across his mouth, but it did little to erase the signs of eating as many figs as he'd put in the bag.

Nadeem scrubbed at his own mouth with his shirttail. "I'm not going."

"You have to, silly. Everyone has to go. The Turks don't ask—they give orders. Isn't it exciting? If they take us, we'll get to see the whole world. We'll go places no one's ever been."

"Not no one. There's people there or the soldiers wouldn't go."

"But they're not people like us. They talk gibberish, and I heard they have tails, and . . . " Nadeem didn't hear the rest because their mother's call sent them racing to the house. Nadeem worried when he saw how pale Mama's face was, but Amer was too excited to notice.

"The Turks are coming, Mama. We heard the drum from the fig

tree. We're going, aren't we, Mama?"

"Yes, we're going." Amer ran and hugged his mother, so he didn't see the tears in her eyes.

Nadeem saw the tears, and his fear grew to a lump in his stomach. "Can I stay home with Hala?"

"No. Hala already left with Papa. No one can stay home. The soldiers will ride all over the valley. If they find anyone in a house, they burn it down."

"What about Grandmother? She can't walk to the village. Will they burn her house? Maybe it won't burn because it's made of stone."

"Papa took the donkey. He'll get Grandmother and meet us at the village."

Papa always thought of everything. Hala was too little to walk all the way to the village, and Mama was too big with child to carry her that far. Mama was shoving bread, cheese, olives, and other kitchen things into a bag. "I don't know how long we'll be gone. Nadeem, you carry this. Amer, get some warm clothes in case we have to stay all night."

Mama hurried them out the door in front of her. They hadn't walked any farther than the almond tree when she told them to wait a minute. She ran back to the house for "one more thing."

Amer took advantage of the pause to continue talking about the Turks. "Have you ever seen their uniforms? They're wool with bright brass buttons. They'll keep you really warm in the winter. And they give everyone boots to keep their feet warm, too. Great shiny leather boots."

"And in the summer you'll cook inside that wool uniform and melt right into those leather boots that raise blisters on your feet."

"It's only just starting autumn. By summer the war'll be over and I'll come home."

"They also give you a sword and a gun."

"Yeah. Isn't it great?"

"No. They expect you to use them."

"Yeah. They'll teach me to shoot—with my own gun."

"Amer." Nadeem stamped his foot. His brother could be so aggravating. "You'll have to shoot other people—and they'll be shooting at you. You could get killed."

"They won't be people like us. They'll be those funny people with tails and maybe even horns. It'll be like killing a chicken." The loud squawk of a frightened chicken made both boys laugh.

Mama came back, carrying a sack. "We might need more food." There was a muffled squawk from the sack. "We can bring her back if we don't need her."

Half a mile toward the village, they saw Papa. He was holding the reins of the donkey with Grandmother and Hala on top. Papa waved and waited for them. The family walked another two miles, joining the trickle of families walking toward the village. Papa walked with his arm around Mama, and they talked in low tones. Nadeem thought Mama was crying, but when he tried to get close enough to hear, Grandmother grabbed his sleeve and made him walk next to her. Amer had already run ahead.

"Grandmother, how come the Turks can tell us what to do? Even the village mokhtar doesn't do that. He settles arguments and stuff, but he doesn't order us around."

"Sometimes he does."

"That's only when he's collecting taxes, and that's for the Ottomans, too." Grandmother was quiet so long that Nadeem started talking again. "Amer said killing people in the war would be like killing chickens because they aren't like us."

Grandmother gave such a big sigh that Nadeem looked to see if she was having trouble breathing, like she did last year. No, it was just a sigh. "That's at the bottom of it all, child. The Turks are pretty good to us as long as we pay the taxes, but in the end—we aren't Turks."

Nadeem took a couple of minutes to think about that. "So they're the Turks and we're the chickens." He scuffed up dust from the dirt road. It probably wouldn't rain until next month. "I think Amer wants to be a Turk."

Grandmother chuckled. "Amer's a very stubborn youngster. If he wants it badly enough, who knows? He might find a Turkish wife to help him along." She reached out and tousled Nadeem's wavy black hair. "And what about you? Do you want to be a Turk?"

"No. I want to stay and help Papa with the farm. He'll need more help when the new baby comes." Nadeem watched the small puffs of dust that swirled around the donkey's hooves. Life without Amer wouldn't be as much fun. Hala was too little to climb trees, and she was just a girl anyway. "Grandmother, Amer'll still be Palestinian, won't he? Even if he puts on a Turkish uniform, he'll always be Palestinian."

"Palestinian, Greater Syrian, Arab. He can't change his blood."

"So he'll always be my brother."

"Of course."

Satisfied, Nadeem skipped ahead. There was a mulberry tree just around the bend. If they were lucky, there might still be some ripe mulberries to pick. As Nadeem hoisted himself onto a low branch, Amer's voice above him said, "Don't bother. The mulberries are all gone."

"I should've known you'd be here," said Nadeem with a laugh as he dropped out of the tree to the purple-stained dirt beneath it. Amer landed next to him, and they waited for the family to catch up. The drum beat was louder now.

When they entered the village, the first house they passed belonged to the widow Um Tariq. The boys were surprised to see half a dozen horses standing in the yard. Um Tariq was shouting, "Just keep those horses away from my spinach patch." They could hear men laughing inside the house. Um Tariq waved at them to stop. She ran over and asked if she could stay with Grandmother. "There might not be anything left by the time they leave, but I'm not staying in the house with those louts."

Another group of soldiers stood in the road, blocking their progress. They ordered the women to go off to the left, and the men to go straight. Nadeem was leading the donkey, and he started to the left. The soldier grabbed the back of his shirt and pointed in the other direction. Nadeem grabbed Papa's hand. Amer already had the other hand. Together they walked toward the center of the village.

It looked very different from the quiet village Nadeem had known all his life. It was noisy with men shouting over the sound of the drum and horses snorting and stamping—more horses than Nadeem had ever seen.

The three joined a group of men and boys from the village. The group got larger as the day moved toward afternoon. Nadeem's head throbbed in time to the incessant drum beat, and his stomach growled in counterpoint. Even Amer's excitement faded.

The drum stopped, and Nadeem thought for a moment that he'd gone deaf. Then he heard the horses again, and a baby cried in the distance. Amer elbowed him and pointed to the mokhtar's house. Standing in the doorway was a tall Turkish soldier, resplendent in a uniform with gleaming brass buttons and gold braid on his epaulets. Shiny black boots reached his knees, and a helmet with a brass ornament on top added even more inches to his frame. He studied the crowd from beneath his dark bushy eyebrows as he turned his stern face with the thick moustache from one side to the other. He looked very grand with his bandoliers across his chest.

"See?" whispered Amer. "I told you they had nice boots."

"But only the Pasha Effendi gets to wear them. Look at everyone else." Amer ignored his words.

The officer nodded at his men. He took a slender stick from his belt and held it against the wall of the mokhtar's house. One of the soldiers ran up with a half-burned branch. Using the charred end, the soldier drew a line on the house where the officer's stick pointed. A sound like the buzzing of a hive of angry bees arose from the village men, and the soldiers moved a little closer. No one said anything out loud. Papa put an arm around the shoulder of each of his boys and pulled them close. Nadeem wanted to ask what was happening, but it didn't seem the right time to talk.

The officer gave an order, and the soldier standing next to him shouted, "All you men form a single line," in strangely accented Arabic. Other soldiers began pushing and shoving the men into line. The mokhtar brought a chair and small table out to the yard, and the officer sat and crossed his legs. The mokhtar went back in the house and came out with a tray holding a brass coffee pot and a small cup. He placed these on the table next to the officer before going back inside.

Nadeem watched as the men were marched, one by one, past the line on the wall. Only a few boys were pulled out of line and sent away. It didn't take long for Nadeem to understand that only the boys shorter than the mark on the wall were sent away. He clutched his father's shirt. "Everyone?" He forced the word past lips paralyzed with fear. They couldn't take everyone—what would the village do? Everyone meant Papa, too. He looked at the men around him. He knew almost all of them by name, and the boys some of them held close. What would their families do without them? What would Mama do? How would Grandmother live all alone?

Old Abu-Mustafa reached the front of the line, leaning on his stick. The soldier snatched the cap off his head and showed his nearly bald head with its fringe of white hair. Then he made him open his mouth. The officer frowned, and the soldiers sent Abu-Mustafa away like the small boys.

Soon it would be their turn. Nadeem tried to swallow. He couldn't slouch low enough to get below the mark. Neither could Amer, but Amer didn't want to. If they took Papa and Amer, there would be no one to help Mama. He had to get away from the soldiers and stay with Mama. But how could he? There were soldiers everywhere.

A shot rang out behind them. Had the soldiers shot someone? The officer shouted orders and everyone, soldiers and villagers alike, started toward the shot. This was his chance. He could run faster than anyone in the village. Maybe he could run and hide until they left. He had to try.

He slipped out from his father's arm and started running. He ran past the mokhtar's house. He ran past the next house and turned away from the road. It was a full six seconds before he heard a shout behind him. He ran behind the next house and he heard more shouts and the pounding of boots. He looked around wildly for a place to hide. They'd find him in no time if he hid in a house. There were no trees he could climb, nothing he could hide behind.

Then he spotted the well. He could hide in the well until the soldiers were gone. The pounding boots were getting closer. He moved the heavy wooden cover aside just enough to squeeze through. He lowered himself into the well, feeling for toe holds in the cracks between the stones lining the well. His heart, already pounding, stepped up the beat as voices approached. He had to get out of sight.

His toes finally worked their way between stones, and he reached up with one arm to slide the cover back in place. It didn't budge. His breath came in short gasps of sheer terror. His toes protested holding his weight, but he had no choice. He needed both arms for the job. Exerting all of his strength, he managed to slide it almost closed. He used all of his strength for one last desperate effort, and the lid dropped into place. The sudden movement shifted his weight and one of the stones beneath his toes moved.

Then the unthinkable happened—his foot slipped, and he plunged down through the darkness. The shock of the icy water cut his scream short. Fear turned his arms into windmills. He choked and sputtered as he flailed in the inky wet prison of the well. What had he done? He'd surely drown. He'd never been in water deeper than Mama's washtub. He'd traded one death for another.

Pain lanced up his leg as his kicking foot hit the side of the well. Sobered by the intensity of the pain from his probably broken toe, Nadeem stopped flailing. Kicking and bobbing, he felt for cracks in the walls. It may have been minutes, but it felt like hours before he discovered that the water didn't quite cover his head. It had been a long, dry summer. If he stood on the tips of his toes, he could breathe. Except for the pain in his toe, he managed to stand quite easily by resting one hand on the wall.

Nadeem's heart skipped a beat when he heard the cover scrape against the stones overhead. The sunlight was blinding after so long in complete darkness, but it showed the outline of a Turkish army headdress. Nadeem tried to call for help. Even the Turkish army would be better than a slow death in the freezing water of the well. He drew in breath to holler for help, but the cover slammed back in place before a sound escaped.

Seconds ticked into minutes, and possibly hours. Nadeem had no way of measuring time. Cold occupied his thoughts. The cold water seemed to be pulling all the warmth from his body. He was sure if the soldiers opened the lid again, they'd hear his teeth chattering before he called for help.

He explored his prison by feel. The stones had been fitted together with expertise, allowing few cracks large enough for fingers or toes. The walls were rough, except below the water line where they felt a little slimy. The well was narrower down here, too. He could brace his feet against one wall and his back against the other. That relieved him from having to stand on tiptoes to breathe.

It had been past lunchtime when the soldiers lined them up. Nadeem figured he had already missed another meal. It must be dark outside. Could he climb out of the well? Would it be safe to try? Maybe not. He'd wait.

Nadeem tried to count minutes, but not only was that boring, but he kept losing track of how many minutes he counted. How long would the soldiers stay? Mama had packed food and brought a chicken in case they stayed longer. How long could he wait without food? He could starve to death.

Hours passed, at least Nadeem thought that hours had passed. His hands and feet were losing feeling. If he was going to climb out, he'd better do it while he could still feel the cracks between the stones. He started up, feeling carefully for the best places for his fingers. His sore toe still hurt, but it worked as well as the others. Slowly he inched his way up the sheer wall of the well. It was a lot harder than climbing a tree, especially in the dark. The rough stones scraped the skin off his fingers. Moving one hand and then one foot at a time was slow work. His arms ached and a painful cramp in one foot made him stop for several minutes, supported by the other foot and hanging by the tips of his fingers.

How high was he? How much farther did he have to climb? It was too dark to see anything. He prayed he'd reach the top soon. His fingertips were getting numb with cold, and the ache in his arms turned to agony. He put the fingers of one hand in his mouth to warm it and get the feeling back. It tasted of blood. Without warning, the stone beneath one foot came out of the wall, leaving him hanging by one hand and his injured foot. Before he could find a crack for the other hand, another stone moved and he fell back into the water.

Back on the bottom, Nadeem tried to restore feeling to his bleeding fingers. Maybe he could go up, keeping his back on one wall and his feet on the other. His hands could help him slide his back up the wall an inch at a time, while his feet kept him steady. He hadn't gone far when his leg muscles began shaking with fatigue. Not long after that, as he put all his weight on his feet to move his body upward, the muscles refused to hold his weight, dumping him once more to the bottom of the well. This time he got a nasty bump on his head before landing.

That's when the tears started. With nobody to witness his humiliation, there was no sense in keeping them bottled up anymore. He was going to die down here in the dark. It didn't matter if he cried like a little baby or screamed like a girl. No one could hear him. He cried until he thought he'd run out of tears. His sobs gradually faded away, leaving him exhausted.

He was hungry, cold, and so tired he wouldn't have been able to stand on his own feet without the water making him lighter. What if he fell asleep? He'd probably drown. Would he die of hunger first? He wondered how long it would take him to die. He was a total fool. If there'd been any chance of escape, the older men would've run away.

He jerked his head up with a start, coughing and choking on water. He must have dozed off. His eyes must have closed without him noticing. After all, it didn't make a lot of difference if they were open or closed in the bottom of the dark well.

No one knew where he was. No one would think of looking in

here. He wondered if Mama knew he hadn't gone with the Turks. Were the Turks gone yet? Papa must be really sad. He knew Papa didn't want to go and leave Mama alone.

Yeah, that's why he'd run in the first place. He couldn't give up now and leave the family without anyone to take care of them. Now at least they'd have him to lean on. He thought about the other families, the ones without older boys. What would they do? How could the village survive?

He had to stay awake. Someone was bound to come for water. Once the Turks left, people would move back to their houses, and someone would need water. All he had to do was stay awake.

He sang songs; he told himself scary stories of jinn and efreet, but he couldn't make up stories as scary as the Turks coming and taking away all the men in the village. He hollered for help until his throat was raw. His voice got quieter and quieter, but he kept going. He had to keep going for Mama and the village. He pounded the walls to warm his hands and the pain of the rough stone kept him from sleeping. The more he thought about the village and what the Turks were doing outside his well, the angrier he got. He'd never forget this day and what the Turks did to them, and he'd never forgive the Ottomans. All he had to do was stay awake.

And then, it happened. Blinding sunlight poured into the well before it was partially blocked by a bucket. The bucket landed in front of him, and it took all of his strength to grab it. His arms didn't want to move, and his hands were dead things with no feeling.

"Help. Help me, please." He wasn't sure his weak cries could be heard from the top of the well, but he hung on to the bucket as hard as he could. He heard a sound, and then nothing. Had the person been frightened and run away? Tears threatened, but he held them back. "Help me." He tried again.

"Who's down there?" A man's deep voice echoed down the well.

Did that mean the Turks were still here? No matter, he couldn't hold on any longer. "It's me, Nadeem."

"Can you hold on to the bucket?"

"I'll try." He couldn't. He dropped back down before they'd pulled him halfway up.

The man came back with a rope with a loop on the end. "Put this under your arms. We'll go slow." Despite their best efforts, Nadeem got a few more bumps and bruises on his way up, but he didn't mind. Hands lifted him over the edge of the well, and he had a fleeting thought of how wonderful it was to be in the sun before he lost consciousness.

Nadeem woke up wrapped in a blanket. He didn't know whose house he was in, but it looked like a village house, and he didn't see any soldiers. He sat on the edge of the bed and clutched the blanket as he realized he wasn't wearing anything under it. "Is anyone here?"

"Oh, glad to see you're up. Hungry?"

"Abu Khalid! How come you're still here?" The man held up his right hand, swathed in thick bandages.

"I shot myself in the hand."

"That was the shot we heard?"

"Yes. I told them that I was running to enlist, and bringing my own gun to help when I tripped." Abu Khalid gave a deep hearty laugh. "They decided the army would be better off without me."

Nadeem tried to stand up, and fell back on the bed. His legs wouldn't hold his weight, and the room started spinning around him. "I have to get home."

"Not until you can walk. You've been two days in that cold water without food. You're lucky to be alive."

Abu Khalid brought him a bowl of bread soaked in hot sweet

tea. "Sorry there's no milk. The Turks ate our goat before they left."

"I had to stay alive, for Mama and the village. I think it was anger that kept me alive. I'll never forgive them for taking Papa and the others."

"You're a plucky, resourceful kid, Nadeem. Who knows, someday you might even lead the rebellion that rids us of the Turks."

AUTHOR'S NOTE: *This story is a combination of two true stories. An old man in a small village near Ramallah told us what he remembered of "The Big Drum" or World War I. We asked why he called WWI the Big Drum, and he related his memory of how the Turks conscripted the men of his village. His story of the man who hid in a well for two days did not end well. Ironically, the man died of pneumonia soon after his rescue.*

To the story of the man in the well, I added the story of my husband's uncle who shot himself in the hand in a successful attempt to avoid conscription by the Turkish army. Luckily, it healed as well as could be expected, although he lost all movement of his permanently twisted fingers.

THE GIRL WHO STUNK OF SUN

A.J. Kirby

The girl at the post office asked for a bottle of gold label tequila. And in that stuffy place of pick n' mix battered dreams and mouldy old magazine hopelessness, her request seemed almost impossibly exotic. Like when I was a kid and I first heard the fabled words "Knickerbocker Glory."

She asked for gold label tequila. Not just any common or garden tequila; gold label. Gold from the Aztec or Mayan Gods, sparkling in the dust. She was like a young Indiana Jones digging for the secrets of the ages. And what with that ring through her lip and the outdoorsy colour to her skin, she looked like she'd travelled quite some way to get it.

The girl seemed to stink of sun, so unlike the everyday women of the town with their overbearing perfume reek. She somehow smelled of swimming pools, too, and her hair was kinda tatty and wrinkled as though she'd not quite dried it properly after a dip and then left it trailing out the window of her sweet-natured old groover of a camper van. She could have been a surfer who'd taken a wrong turn somewhere back along the road network, or an actress method-acting a surfer, or an actress who surfed in her spare time. She was miles from the sea; miles from anywhere she could legitimately swim but seemed to bring with her something of the liquidity of possibility into the post office.

Into the solid mundanity of Nabil's post office on main street with its stacks of old birthday cards whose messages were so out-of-date they'd come back into fashion, in an ironical kind of way. Into Nabil's where one stray step too close to the back counter and its wall of variety-pack envelopes could bring about a volley of barking from the dogs in the tiny yard behind the back door. Into Nabil's where cans of beans were priced at over a pound and where *everything stopped* at a quarter past twelve when his wife always brought out his sandwiches and his cup of hot sweet tea.

"Gold label tequila," she repeated. "The good stuff."

Oh I imagined it was the good stuff, all right. I imagined it contained flecks of real gold and the taste of ambrosia. I imagined drinking it would colour everything with some golden glow of endless wonder.

Behind her in the queue, and two in front of me, an old crone tutted and clutched her *Loyal Companion Weekly* closer to her chest as though she feared that even the mention of tequila would turn the girl all-renegade. No doubt the old crone's only conception of renegade was somebody else trying to take the final copy of *her* magazine; there was probably no doubt in her mind that it was *her* magazine. She looked the type that would get the people at the *foreign shop* to order it in especially for her, and what's more, she looked the type that wouldn't pay the extra few coins to get it delivered. I imagined her facing the same agonising trip down to the shopping parade every week; every week she'd hardly be able to keep up with her tartan trolley as she desperadoed to the shop, *sure* that this would be the week that some renegade bandit had stolen her *Loyal Companion*.

I could read the people in the queue like a particularly well-thumbed book. Like a TV magic-man I could discern the nuances of their lives, only, in a place like Newton Mills, it wasn't such a skill. Here, everyone's lives were monochrome. Here, the girl couldn't have stood out more if she'd been a goddamn luminous space invader.

"Tequila. Gold Label," she said again. The girl was beautiful in a take-no-prisoners kind of way. Bristling with a sense of other-worldly confidence that seemed out of place in the drab surroundings. I could only see her side-on, but already, she looked like a dream. A dream of something better, less conventional than Newton Mills and all of its decay.

Behind the counter, Nabil eyed the girl with distaste. He looked like he didn't like working behind the counter. Looked like he hated it, in fact. Looked like he thought the whole point of building up a business empire was so *he* didn't have to do the dirty work of peddling booze to the borderline under-aged and desperate alcoholics banned from the cheaper supermarket up the road. But his usual helper, Mrs. Dawson, had most likely called in sick (again), and so here he was. Once upon a time, the post office had been exactly that; a post office. But the *real money* was in booze, or so some wise man in passing had probably told him, and so he'd branched out. And now he probably couldn't remember the last time he'd sold anything remotely resembling a stamp.

"How old are you?" asked Nabil. The girl was plenty old enough. One look at her and I knew she was old enough. Something about the way she held herself. But Nabil had evidently taken an instant dislike to her and her alien confidence and was throwing up any stumbling block that he possibly could just so he could dent her armour, send her away with a bit less of a bounce in her step. Nobody in Newton Mills had a bounce in their step.

The girl shook off the question with a neat shrug of the shoulders. The man's check-shirt she was wearing slipped off her shoulder, exposing a wonderful bra-strap and lovely honeyed skin. "I'd like a bottle of gold label tequila," she repeated.

"And I asked how old are you?" repeated the shopkeep.

In the queue, the old crone tutted once again, or maybe she simply adjusted her false teeth. The man in work overalls bent his head in a way that vaguely suggested that he was losing patience. The air was full of muted impatience. But the girl didn't sense it. She didn't sense any of it. She wanted her tequila. She wanted her tequila on a Sunday afternoon and no less. Nobody in Newton Mills drank tequila. Let alone on a Sunday. The very idea seemed to whisper *freedom* to me.

"I'm plenty old enough to take a drink, pardner," said the girl with a smile. And again, she pointed up at the high-shelves teeming with booze behind the counter; shelves that wouldn't have looked out of place in an old-school library with one of those wheeled-ladders to help the librarian get around. I'd once seen Mrs. Dawson climb precariously up on the third shelf up so she could reach a particularly tricky vodka. Perhaps that explained her absence. Perhaps she'd mountaineered for alcohol one too many times.

Nabil shook his head wearily. Three or four of his chins continued to shake long after he'd stopped. A Wild West stand-off appeared to be developing, and I had my usual to buy. I couldn't really afford the delay; I was illegally parked outside after all. And I knew deep down that it would be better to simply slip back out the door and up to the supermarket where I could purchase my Dorchester and Greys and my Sunday paper for about half the price they were in Nabil's, and probably in half the time. But my interest was piqued.

The girl simply smiled, repeated her question and waited.

Behind me, the little bell jangled to indicate that someone else had entered the shop. I looked round to see a tracksuit-clad teenager. He was wearing that same look which fused seething violence and total incomprehension that all of the youngsters in the town seemed to have down pat. He selected a can of pop from the fridge and joined the queue behind me. Nabil, I knew, prided himself on his short queues, and this was the longest I'd ever seen it. Soon it would be snaking out the door if either he or the girl didn't budge.

"No ID, no sale," he said. "Look, duck; there's a queue developing"—as though queue was somehow a synonym for *situation* or *disaster*— "and other people want to get served. If you cannot show me proof of age, then you take away no tequila today."

"Tequila makes me happy," said the girl.

Nabil nodded. "ID makes me happy."

"Oh, serve the girl," said the man in work overalls. "Let her have the tequila. She looks *of age* to me . . . Look at her." The way he said this, innocent as it seemed, seemed to drip with sleaze.

"Just show the man some ID, love, so we can all get on with the rest of our days," said the old crone, thrusting her *Loyal Companion* out in front of her. *That* was the rest of her day.

The girl looked back at the queue for the first time. Shrugged apologetically. "I don't actually carry identification," she said. "I'm just me and that's the way I like it."

I liked it too. Nobody else did; I could feel the prickle of violence in the hairs at the back of my neck. The sudden determination of the majority of the people in the post office that this girl had somehow over-stepped the mark; her show of wilfulness had gone on for too long,   and now she had to be taught a small-town lesson.

"Get her out of here," snarled the overall-man in front of me. I heard him crack his knuckles. Saw the bristling "hate" tattoo contorting on his fist. "This has gone too far."

"Yeah, chuck her out," grunted the tracksuited teenager. He was fiddling with something in his pocket now. Perhaps a knife.

"No ID, no sale," muttered the old crone, her *Loyal Companion* now rolled up into a tube as though she were about to swat a particularly troublesome fly with it.

Nabil listened to the dissent from his customers and sneered back at the girl, who for the first time seemed a little uneasy. Her confidence had been shaken.

She pointed again. A slight tremble in her finger this time. "Look, I don't want to be any trouble. I can see the bottle right up there on the fourth shelf. Right in the middle, next to the Ouzo. Just let me have a bottle and I'll be out of your hair."

Nabil didn't have much hair to speak of. Not on the top of his head, on which it was closely cropped and kinda shiny in the artificial light. Evidently he didn't have any patience to speak of either. He slammed his fist down onto the counter, causing some of the packets of football stickers to slip out of their display stand. The old crone in front of me jumped in alarm. "Not today," he said. "Get out of my shop."

I should have stepped in then, offered to pay for the bottle before everything got messy. I should have spoken up. Let it be known that Nabil had no need to worry; none of us would say anything to the authorities if he allowed the girl her prize. Or let it be known that he was treating her badly; that there was no way she was under-age in any case and that he was just being an old stick in the mud. But I remained tight-lipped as I always do. I kept my head off the parapet so nobody could fire at it. I let the girl face what she had to face.

In a place like Newton Mills, where everyone hates everyone else, keeping that undercurrent of violence from bubbling up and overwhelming everything was a difficult, some might say impossible, task. But when an outsider was thrown into the mix, everything changed. Suddenly it became all Newton Mills together; old enmity was thrust aside. The honour of the town was at stake and the residents became like brothers again. I noticed Nabil's slight nod, first to the overall-man and then to the tracksuited teenager. Their wordless agreement on *something*. That the overall-man had probably come in here, dripping with racism every other day of the calendar year meant nothing now. That the tracksuited teenager had most likely attempted to steal from the shop on his every visit was meaningless.

My eyes darted to the girl, who was now edging slightly away from the counter. Her face had suddenly flushed. She returned my gaze, appealing for my help. *Asking* me to step in. To do something. I looked away. Out of the corner of my eye, I watched the tracksuited teenager slouch on over to the front door and quickly slam the lock home. Then he turned the sign in the window from "open" to "closed."

"Wh—what's going on?" stuttered the girl.

Nobody answered her.

"Why have you locked the door?" she asked, this time more forcefully. "What are you . . . "

Nabil turned his back, reached up to the fourth shelf and picked out the dusty bottle of gold label tequila. It no longer looked like freedom or like Aztec Gold. It looked like a reserve weapon. Carefully, he placed the bottle on the counter and then he smiled. A gap-toothed, grave-stone smile that told me everything I needed to know about what was going to happen.

"Come get the thing," said Nabil. "If you dare."

The girl seemed in two minds what to do. She half-stepped towards the counter and then kinda lurched away again. As she did so, the old crone stuck out her tartan trolley and the girl collapsed right over it and onto the black and white chequered tiles on the floor. The girl's beautiful eyes blazed right open with terror, right up from the floor.

"Who the hell do you think you are?" asked the overall-man, looming over her. And then he hawked up a mouthful of saliva and snot. He opened his mouth and the whole unholy mix started to dribble out from between his teeth. A great globule of it—egg-yolk yellow—trailed down in a slow, unbroken stream towards the girl's face. She opened her mouth to scream and then thought better of it. To scream would be to invite the man's snot into her mouth. She tried to roll off to the side, but the tracksuited teenager saw what she was about to do and clamped a multi-coloured trainer-clad foot on her shoulder. The girl gave out a little whimper of fear. And then of disgust as the overall-man's saliva landed on her finally. She let it run off her cheek like a spattering of mustard-mayonnaise.

Nabil came out from behind the counter, wielding a baseball bat. He'd wrapped tubi-grip on the handle so it wouldn't hurt his goddamn palms when he swung it. And I knew I should step in then. I knew that I should play the voice of reason. Knew that I *had to*. Otherwise, the scene would only get worse. But I couldn't move. I felt like I'd grown roots—what was it my old mother used to say about standing in queues for too long?

"No!" screamed the girl as soon as she caught sight of Nabil's baseball bat. "No no no no no no."

Nabil clutched the baseball bat in both hands and raised it above his head, exposing terrible sweat patches under his arms. His shirt was pretty much wringing wet there, like he'd been swimming.

"Wait!" called the old crone. "Hold your horses, chief."

Nabil lowered his arms. Looked disappointed.

"What?" asked overall-man, running a meaty hand through his messy hair.

"Well . . . be careful, that's all. I mean, we don't want all the hassle of the questions if we kill her, do we? Can you imagine all the time they'd waste?" She looked forlornly at her *Loyal Companion*.

"She's right, you know," said Nabil, thoughtfully. "Remember that

Australian that went in the chippy on New Street? They had to close the place down for a month after they fished his feet out of the fryer."

The girl let out this terrified yelp. The tracksuited teenager moved his foot away from her shoulder and jammed it in her mouth.

"We can't just let her up and out of here though . . . She'll talk," said overall-man.

"I won't talk . . . I won't say anything to anyone," said the girl through a mouthful of multicoloured trainer.

And suddenly all of them turned to me. Four sets of black, soulless eyes. And *her* eyes. Her beautiful green eyes.

"What do you think?" asked Nabil. "You haven't said nothing so far, Mr. Coverley."

What did I think? What did I make of this madness?

"Well?" asked the old crone, staring at my speechless mouth.

"Come on," said the tracksuited teenager. "We haven't got all day."

I stared back at them all, at the girl on the floor, back at them, at the girl on the floor with the spit all over her face and back at them with their barbed-wire faces and their cement-mixer mouths. My palms sweated like they'd never done before, my heart jungle-drummed in my chest. The girl looked back at me with *promise* in her eyes. The old crone seethed with anger; I wasn't like the good old boys from her day. Boys whose stories still filled the pages of *Loyal Companion*. Boys who would go off to war and fight for what was theirs. The tracksuited teenager was disgusted; Nabil uncomprehending.

Without really knowing what I was doing, I plunged forward and out of my reverie. I knocked overall-man out of the way and into the discounted chocolate bar display. Tracksuited-teenager was skittled towards the local newspapers and the old crone staggered backwards into the open drinks fridge. Only Nabil stood firm. Fat Nabil with his baseball bat.

"You cannot behave like this in my establishment," he said, swinging his bat from side to side.

I knew I couldn't. I had already overstepped the mark. Already made *myself* a target. So there was no turning back. I edged towards him, creeping ever closer so that the wind from his swinging bat brushed against my ears. I edged towards him, uttering this low, bestial growl of warning. Overall-man, the tracksuited teenager, and the old crone remained pressed against the wall. Even Nabil seemed a little perturbed by my apparent madness. And I *was* mad. It was truly a life-defining moment. A moment which hung in the air like a piñata, waiting to explode. Waiting to shower the little golden baubles of fate wherever they may land.

But then I heard the click of the lock and the tinny jangle of the small bell on the door. I spun round to see the flash of a man's shirt exiting the shop, the ragtag of her hair. The girl had escaped. Somehow while Nabil and I squared-up to each other, she had taken it upon herself to clamber to her feet and make for the door. And she'd made it. Miraculously, she'd made it. She left behind her this powerful lingering smell of sun and water.

"You let her get away," snarled Nabil, advancing on me once again.

"No ... I ... "

The bat whizzed past my ear.

"You let her escape."

The bat was somehow even closer this time as it whirled past my head. And I knew that I had to follow the girl. Get out. Make for the old Volvo which was illegally parked outside—I'd only thought I'd be in the post office for a minute at the very most, officer—and drive. Drive away from these people, this soulless town, this violent mundanity.

Now, Nabil and I were walking round in vicious circles, orbiting each other like murderous moons. I jarred my hip on the counter as I circled past and reached out for something to use as a weapon . . . the first thing that came to hand.

The first thing that my fingers closed around was the square bottle of gold label tequila. The gold of Newton Mills. Barely allowing myself a moment to think, I launched the bottle at Nabil's head and then ran. I heard the smash and his muted, terrified scream as I pushed through the door. Then I heard that little jangle-bell and knew I was on the way to safety. I didn't look back.

* * *

I drove up out of town on the road that intersected Mossman Park. Trees flanked the roads, and I kept thinking that I saw mad Nabil in the shadows, blood a-spurting from his face. I couldn't stop my hands from trembling on the wheel and kept drifting over to the wrong side of the road. And yet somehow, fear was not my over-riding emotion. Somehow, the sense of *loss* hung heaviest with me; a massive, weighty disappointment. When I'd first heard the girl ask for the gold label tequila, she'd offered me a glimpse of a better, sunnier life, but now she had left, she'd taken with her all possibility, all hope of my ever living in that world. Now she'd left, she had left me empty and worse off than before. Worse than I'd been in my narrow, stilted existence, because now I knew what was on the other side of the curtain.

I drove on, hearing the Volvo coughing and spluttering under me like a sick horse. And I absently wondered what had happened to the girl and whether she was okay. Whether she'd lose that spring in her step as a result of what had happened to her.

And then I saw her, way out ahead, ambling along the pathway, head in the clouds. It had to be her, swinging her small bag over her shoulder like that. As I drew closer, I took in the man's shirt and the honeyed colour of her skin. That hair. And I'm sure that if I'd have wound down the window, I would have smelled the sea.

71

On a whim, I pulled up alongside her and stopped the car, sensing that perhaps *this* would be my last chance of a golden future. The girl carried on walking. Ignored me. I climbed out of the Volvo and hurried after her, not quite knowing what name I should use to call her back. Or whether she'd even have a name at all; she didn't look the type for labels of any description.

"Hey!" I shouted. "Hey you!"

Finally she turned. Looked at me quizzically. I suddenly realised that she did not recognise me. And what's more, I hardly recognised her either. She looked young. Too young to have been the girl of my dreams in the post office. Too young to be asking for gold label tequila. For a moment, I stood there, sheepish.

"What?" she breathed, in the manner of a peevish teen. "What do you want?"

"The post office . . . " I muttered.

It was clear that she didn't have the slightest clue as to what I was talking about. My eyes tried to seek out the left-over saliva on her apple-red cheek, the lip-ring. I couldn't seem to find either.

"Whatever," said the girl, gesturing off over her shoulder. I didn't understand what she was doing.

"The post office?"

She gestured again. And then I realised that she was pointing me *in the direction* of the post office, as though I was asking her where it was.

"No matter," I said. "Tell you what; why don't I drive you down to the supermarket where I can pick up a bottle of gold label tequila for you?"

"Why on earth would you want to buy me tequila?" asked the girl.

"Not just any tequila . . . Gold label tequila . . . "

"Whatever," said the girl, chewing furiously on her gum. "Get back in your car, paedo."

And then she started to drift away from me. I collapsed down onto the ground and watched her as she went. And soon, I couldn't pick her out amongst the fallen leaves. Soon she became just a golden glow, like everything else. Soon, she was gone.

Jailface

Lindsay A. Chudzik

I've read the first night in prison is the worst, but I'm optimistic. I adopt jailface, another thing I've read about. Jailface means putting on an appearance that says I'm dead inside, projecting that nothing or no one can break me because I've already been broken. Criminals are drawn to rosy cheeks and upturned grins, to clutched purses and quickened steps. Criminals are drawn to people who seem like they have something to lose.

"Last night Ron set my hair on fire. My boyfriend," my cellie, Tess, explains when she notices my staring. Hair's dead by definition, the cells within each strand no longer living once they reach the skin's surface, but her hair looks charred. Tess resembles a bartender I knew once, terrible tattoos she sketched herself covering her arms and calves. I feel bad critiquing her tattoos this way, but it's easier than thinking about her burnt ponytail and what her strawberry blonde hair might have looked like before it was set ablaze. Before she met her boyfriend. Before she dropped out of high school. Before she had to attend one of the worst schools in the state.

"Sorry," I say.

"For what?" Tess asks. She shoves her head under the sink's

spigot in the corner of our holding cell. Rusty water mixed with ash pools in its metallic bowl. Our other two cellies don't comment.

"It's sad about your hair," I say. I think of how I chopped off all of my hair in the eleventh grade so I could change its color and style with the switch of a wig when leaving school. A black beehive. A cotton candy pink bob. Dirty blonde dreadlocks. I hate how Tess has been pushed into her new hair, though, and I wish I had my box of wigs to offer.

I examine the bottoms of my feet. Black. The guards made us leave our shoes outside our cell. "The laces could be used for hangings," the guard said. "And those heels could be used as weapons." He pointed to my brand new BCGB pumps, then tugged at strands of his Fu Manchu. If I were going to gouge someone's eyes out with my shoes, I probably wouldn't have spent so much time searching for designer brands on clearance racks. But that would entail premeditation and the guards seem to understand that most of these women act on impulse, rather than weighing their options. It seemed even more than that. These women didn't have options to weigh. Their lives were a game of action and reaction. Things were done to them. They did things back. Somewhere along the way, perhaps at birth, the word "choice" was removed from their vocabularies.

"Send me an angel," Tess sings while ringing out what's left of her hair. Her voice is gravely and she hits just one note. "That's my favorite song. I love 80's shit."

"I remember roller skating to that song," I say. Tess nods. I think of the rink's DJ, some guy named Johnny who my friends and I thought was the coolest. It occurs to me now that he was a guy in his thirties who pedaled glow-in-the-dark necklaces to children. A guy in his thirties who wore a Michael Jackson glove and only stepped out of his booth to demonstrate his fancy footwork on the rink during power ballads.

It also occurs to me that, although Tess looks much older, she's probably about my age. If we grew up in the same town, I might have hung out with her friends or she might have hung out with mine. We might've drooled over Johnny together and helped each other reapply our apricot-flavored lip-gloss in front of the dingy bathroom mirror.

"I deserved it," Tess says, more to herself. She rolls up the sleeves of her stained Virginia Tech sweatshirt. Since we're in a holding cell, we don't get orange jumpsuits yet. Even though it's sleeting outside, inside it feels like the worst part of summer.

"I stole his car. He loves that Mazda more than anyone. What you in for?"

"Theft," another cellie, Desiree, answers instead. She jumps from the top bunk. She tells us she's a cosmetologist and that she wanted to apply make-up one last time before turning herself in. The foundation, rouge, lip and eyeliner might last until she's forced to take her first shower. I'm told that could be days. She resembles a drag queen, though I'm not sure if this is because of her muscular stature or because of the way her make-up is applied. My mother would call it "war paint" and talk badly about the types of girls who used cosmetics this way.

I push my back against the cinderblock wall, then slide down it until my bottom meets my feet. My gold-speckled cocktail dress is short so I have to be careful how I cross my legs. Since I know I'll eventually have to pee in front of these strangers, I find myself grasping at the few elements of etiquette I can control.

I consider how the backs of my legs will likely be just as black as the bottoms of my feet now, sitting on the concrete floor. I look towards the bunks, but they're only covered with thin, soiled-looking sheets.

"You can ask a guard for a blanket," Tess says, following my gaze. "To sit on. I asked for a book yesterday." She slides me a beaten-up romance novel, though someone scratched out its title. I used to read my mother's Danielle Steeles during summer vacations. The prose was so simple, the situations so predictable, I was certain I could mimic the author's career. I even titled my first novel—Throbbing Manhood. Since I was in the fourth grade and didn't know a great deal about manhood, throbbing or otherwise, I didn't get much further than the title.

I open the book and read, trying to ignore the doodles in the margin. *Fuck Officer Kingsley. Petersberg Posse. Ronald 4eva.* I doubt these readers were ever taught how to annotate a text despite their obvious desire to talk back. Pages 13-34 are ripped from the binding, leaving a sizeable hole in the plot.

"You in for prostitution," Desiree says, locking eyes with me while she guesses my crime. "And you in for drug possession." This time she points to our fourth cellie, a woman I nearly forgot was here. She sits on the other top bunk, rocking, otherwise silent.

"This is crap," Tess says. "I'm gonna miss three weeks of work all 'cause Ron's got a cousin who's a cop."

"Your boyfriend's cousin arrested you?" I ask.

"Ron called him to tell him I was driving his car," Tess says. "On a suspended. But I was just trying to get away from him. To stop fighting, ya know?"

"Will you lose your job?" I ask.

Tess looks at me like this is a stupid question. She never answers it. Instead, she says, "Just have to sleep with that dishwasher at work now. He offered $200 and looks clean. Besides, he can't speak English too well so he can't tell Ron what we do." "You bilingual?" Desiree asks. Tess shakes her head. "How you know he wants to have sex then?"

"Hand gestures," she says, making a circle with her index finger and thumb, then pushing the middle finger from her other hand through it.

"Then he could use hand gestures to tell Ron," Desiree says.

"Good point," I say. "I've known you for less than an hour and I know your boyfriend set your hair on fire. I don't think you're the best judge of character." I stay glued to my spot on the floor and try to look tough, certain Tess will punch or kick me, glad I didn't take it a step further and call her stupid for even considering Ron at this point.

"You're probably right," Tess says instead. "What do you do?"

"I told you," Desiree says. "She a prostitute." Looking around, I realize it's probably unusual for women to wear cocktail dresses and tiaras in Southside Virginia, especially women who land themselves in jail. I doubt most prostitutes dress much differently from the women in my cell and decide these women are just buying into Hollywood stereotypes. I realize I've bought into this myth, too. I think of the pregnant prostitute who used to work the corner of a block where I lived in Philadelphia as an undergraduate. She usually wore spandex and an Eagles sweatshirt. It upset me at the time how little pride she took in her work, how little she looked like Julia Roberts, so much so I almost bought her a pair of fishnets.

"I teach college," I say.

"What you teach?" Desiree asks.

"Writing," I say.

"Then you can help me write an alibi," Desiree says.

"Or she can fill in the missing pages of that book," Tess says to Desiree, pointing to the novel.

"Read the first few pages out loud," Desiree says, speaking to just me as she scoops up the book. "I forget what happens."

"She can't read," Tess tells me.

"Can too," Desiree says. "I'm just lazy."

"I've seen her trying to sound out words," Tess says in a way that sounds more concerned than antagonistic. This makes me like her.

We form a reading semi-circle on the ground, our fourth cellie remaining on the top bunk, sitting Indian-style with her head between her knees. I take it from the top, then start filling in details like a Choose Your Own Adventure book. Tess and Desiree ooh and aah at my authorial decisions. I feel accomplished, like I've finally found the audience for that romance novel I started to pen in the fourth grade.

"Why doesn't someone else take over?" I ask.

I pass the novel to Desiree, but she turns from me. "Nah," she says. "You more charismatic. Charismatic, the way an expert can be."

* * *

First

Blues lights flash in my rearview. I know I was speeding—I'm always speeding—and hope the cop makes this exchange quick because I want to go to bed. I'm on my way home from a trip to Chapel Hill and I'm almost to Richmond, yet far enough to be in the middle of nowhere.

"Any idea how fast you were traveling?" the cop asks. He wears a State Trooper's hat and its large brim casts a shadow over his face, making it impossible for me to make out anything other than his mouth. It's 3 a.m.

"Sure," I say. "I have an idea."

"Eighty in a sixty-five," the officer says. "In Virginia, that's reckless."

"I thought the speed limit was seventy," I say.

"Step out of the vehicle," he says, dismissing my comment. The cop tells me I'm going to have to perform a series of roadside sobriety tests—walk a straight line in six-inch heels while blinded by oncoming traffic, say the alphabet backwards from N to A, name at least four Civil War Generals that fought on the Confederate side. Balance isn't my strong suit, plus I'm a Yankee here on loan for graduate school.

"Can I take off my heels?" I ask.

"No," the officer says. "Too much trash and glass on the shoulder." Since I can't walk in stilettos too well as is, especially brand new stilettos that haven't adjusted to the shapes of my feet and have left blisters on their backs, I teeter and wobble.

"Can I name Revolutionary War heroes instead?" I ask. "Major players in the Vietnam War? A timeline for World War I or II?"

"Confederates," the officer says.

"Robert E. Lee," I say. "Stonewall Jackson. Beauregard." I feel proud of that last one because I seem to pull it out of thin air, recalling a bar called General Beauregard's in Athens, Georgia, and how my friend and I joked that someone should open a place called Sherman's right across the street, giant torches book-ending its doors.

"That's three," the officer says.

"Sherman," I say. I know he's a Yankee. I know he burned Atlanta to the ground, but I don't know anything else to say.

"How much have you had to drink?" the officer asks, forgetting the alphabet bit.

"Just one," I say, a stock response that isn't even true. Since this situation is so unfamiliar, I find myself grasping at clichés.

"Blow into this," the officer says, shoving a device that smells medicinal into my face. After a few seconds, it beeps and he backs away. "Close enough to .08 to take you to the station. Roadside Breathalyzers are crap."

I assume .08 is past the legal limit in Virginia and, even though I feel perfectly sober and capable, I fear this newfangled machine at the station might produce that magic number. He must be certain it will because he shackles my ankles and cuffs my wrists, before pushing me into the back seat of his cruiser. As he snakes through country roads marked by the occasional clapboard shack or trailer, he explains he has to transport me to the jail in the next county over because there are no holding cells for women where we're at. As an afterthought, he decides to read me my Miranda rights from the front seat and, as he goes through each, I have a feeling most of these rights will be violated.

* * *

Later

The guards slide four metal trays through the door. Breakfast. I don't get up, but Tess brings me my meal—runny eggs, white bread, an empty cup to fill with tinny water from the sink in our cell, and an apple with skin that's more brown than green. I pocket the fruit in case lunch is worse, then position the tray by the door.

"You gonna eat those eggs?" Tess asks. "They always give me gas, but if you're not gonna eat them, I want your share." I look towards the toilet a few feet away but, before I can object, Tess is spooning my eggs onto her plate and Desiree descends on our fourth cellie's tray. They don't sample this, then that, dipping their bread into the yolks of their eggs, but instead eat directionally, moving from right to left like the sun moves across the sky. They don't say a word while eating. "You can't save that apple," Tess says once she's finished, reaching into my pocket. "Sorry," she says when she notices me flinch. "But that's considered smuggling contraband. Depending on a guard's mood, saving an apple can add four weeks to your sentence. You better eat it now." I wonder how many times she's been here. Then, it's almost like she reads my mind as she starts in on a list, comparing and contrasting all of the jails and prisons in the region much like I might compare restaurants or rate hotels on Yelp. She explains which have the best and worst food, guards, and showers. She swears this jail is the worst in every category.

The guards corral the trays in five minutes, whether inmates are finished or not.

I think of returning to the romance novel, then consider some of the games my family played on road trips. I don't want to lead in with "I went on vacation and packed something that starts with the letter A" or "I went to the grocery store and bought something that starts with the letter Q." I know we're all hungry to be somewhere else, to taste something better after that wretched prison breakfast. I can't believe after backpacking through Europe and South America, I'm longing for a simple trip to the Piggy Wiggly.

"Let's play word association," I say.

"Word association?" Desiree asks.

"You say a word, then the next person says whatever word comes to mind," Tess explains. "It's easy. My mom made me play in the car during the summer to try to make me forget how hot I was. She refused to put on the AC because she needed the windows down to smoke. Anyhow, rainbow," Tess starts, jumping to her feet, anxious. She tells me she was prescribed Lithium on the outside, but here they make people come off of everything, just like that. She says it feels okay to feel manic and lack focus at times, but that she's encountered some real crazies forced to forfeit their anti-psychotic meds, a prison rule that sometimes leads to things getting pretty dicey. It seems most of the prison rules are designed to make people get worse instead of better. Even though Tess excludes herself from the ways these policies affect her, she tells me how she tried to commit suicide the last time she was incarcerated. She decides she probably just missed her boyfriend too much and couldn't think clearly because of it. She decides the prison psychologist was right, too—that she just wanted attention.

"Grill," Desiree says, bringing us back to our game.

"How you get grill from rainbow?" Tess asks.

"Pot of motherfucking gold," Desiree says. I feel embarrassed because I'd almost blurted George Forman, picturing lean burgers and infomercials instead of blinged-out teeth.

"Kanye West," I say instead. I'd read an article about him wanting to replace his teeth with diamonds.

We look to our fourth cellie who's still on the top bunk. "Crack," she says. Tess tries to keep the game going, offering "Whitney Houston," but once we reach our fourth cellie she offers the same word again, the only image her mind is capable of conjuring.

The guards interrupt our game. They're transferring Desiree to gen pop and she's happy about the move. The tiers have board games, cable TV, and commissary stores, rackets that get poor families to support the prison system. Tess told me these stores even have their own channels to advertise their wares to inmates. She knows it's a scam, but also knows there's nothing else to do here.

"Don't get cable," Tess says to Desiree as she's leaving. "They want you to get the cable, but I got my GED instead last time."

I hand Desiree the tattered romance novel. "Sound out the words. You'll get the hang off it." I hope they'll assign her a reading tutor, put her in some sort of class or workshop. Somehow I convince myself they will because it's easier for this to be my last image of Desiree. Who exactly is stealing from whom is all muddled in my mind and I'm starting to feel like it's the wrong people who end up on the inside.

"That's non-transferable," the guard says, scooping the book out of Desiree's hands as she leaves us.

Our other cellie's withdraw intensifies. She sprawls in front of the toilet, her face resting on its seat while she dry heaves. Tess and I take turns holding back her hair and rubbing her back.

"Can I make my call?" I scream at a passing guard. Initially, they thought I had to stay for eight hours to sober up. Then they thought I was waiting for a bondsman to post my bail. At one point they thought I was Desiree, that I was being charged for stealing from a grocery store.

"Right," he says. "We finally found your file. Not sure why we kept you."

He leads me to a front desk, then I tell him which numbers to dial. "Scottie!" I say too quickly as he hands me the phone. It's still ringing. He answers after four rings. "I was supposed to pick up my dry cleaning," I say, wanting to start the conversation with something small, something familiar. "Could you pick it up? I won't be back to Richmond before five?"

"Where are you?" he asks. When I tell him, he freaks out and says he's on his way.

"We'll come get you when he's here," the guard says, taking away the phone before I've even said goodbye. I'm confused why they don't set me free, but I don't press the issue. If I were permitted to walk out of this jail now, I wouldn't know where to go. I suppose that's the point—isolating inmates from the outside world and from any familial connections as much as possible so that all they know is jail, so that their points of comparison become more and more distant the longer they're here.

"You leaving or what?" Tess asks as the door locks behind me. She barely looks up from the romance novel she's reading again.

"How can you get so into that book?" I ask.

"These people have money and they don't get beat up." I don't know what to say, but luckily she starts talking again. "Your parents must be proud, you being a fancy college teacher and all," she says. My thoughts flash to how disappointed my parents would be right now, though, and how disappointing studying to be a "fancy college teacher" could be as well. Tess and I were saddled with different kinds of debt. Her criminal record would likely hold her back from getting an education, while the debts I incurred from getting an education would likely hold me back from ever living much beyond hand-to-mouth. Still, I recognize paying my student loan officers just means not eating out as much or not buying a house anytime soon. My debts hold less weight.

"I want my kids to be proud of me," Tess says. "That's why I told them I'd be away for job training."

I consider what she's going to tell her kids if she's fired. I figure most restaurants don't hold jobs for people while they're incarcerated. Then I recall my first job in high school. I answered an ad for a waitress and later found out I'd be filling in for a girl while she finished her stint in prison. I trained with a sixteen-year-old whose boyfriend dropped off their two children during her shift because he couldn't find a sitter. I alternated between bringing them coloring books and Shirley Temples. They raced each other to the bottoms of their Shirley Temples, certain the drinks were alcoholic, giddy because they felt let into some secret world and didn't want some adult swiping it away, just like that. They played MASH on the backs of their placemats, fantasizing about living in Los Angles and getting jobs as models or sports agents. At the time, I told myself those kids didn't stand a chance at getting any decent jobs. Feeling bad for them, I convinced the bartender to put the Cartoon Network on the big screen television. I walked outside for a cigarette during my break, then kept walking to my car, leaving my nametag and apron in the parking space beside mine, these artifacts waiting to get rained on or run over by a customer anxious to devour some ribs.

"Maybe I'll take some classes at the community college when I get out," Tess says. "You've got me thinking. I can't be a waitress forever, right?"

For some reason, I believe Tess has a shot, unlike the two kids I chaperoned that afternoon in high school. I can't explain my change in attitude. Perhaps it came with age or perhaps I'm just as bad as most people, incapable of empathizing until I'm forced to because I don't have the choice to walk away. I'm also left with the sinking feeling that, as much as I've wanted to get out of here as quickly as possible, now I wish I had more time with Tess.

* * *

Finally

It's the third time my case is on the docket. The first time the officer was a no show, the second, my public defender, but today I can account for all parties. It's also the third morning of spending hours in front of the mirror, tossing aside countless dresses that hinted at recklessness, finally deciding on an outfit that I hoped screamed innocence. Today that outfit's a plaid jumper, cardigan, Mary Jane flats, and a pearl necklace. I even fashioned my hair into a bun.

The courthouse is packed, so much so the guards rely on walkie-talkies to seat people. Initially, there is only space in the courtroom for those whose cases are being heard. All wives, cousins, and grandmothers are instructed to wait outside. As time passes, spots free up and the guards approach this horde, saying things like they can seat a party of four or just one up front. It takes hours before they deem seating to be general admission.

Since my public defender suggested I accept a plea bargain for a twelve-month license suspension, use of a restricted after the first three, I doubt she understands the logistics of my case. I have a clean driving record, a clean criminal background, and, most importantly, I'm only facing reckless speeding charges since I initially blew a .07. I don't trust her credibility. Her suit needs ironing and she props open a book on her lap that looks like DUI for Dummies. I've heard of defendants accusing cops of having faulty radar guns or detectors, but never of a cop insisting his case should be won because his roadside equipment was shoddy.

"I want to testify," I say lowly, elbowing my public defender while another case is being heard.

"I can ask the officer questions to trip him up maybe," she says. "He didn't record the time of your arrest, which invalidates the results of your Breathalyzer."

"But the results of my Breathalyzer should invalidate this case," I say.

"If we lose, we can take this to the higher court," she says.

"Appeal to Virginia's Supreme Court?" I ask.

"No," she says, confused. "The court on the second floor of this building. If you testify, you'll have to be sworn in. On a Bible."

"I'll take my chances," I say. I quickly learned that, when calling attorneys to potentially hire, they would answer anywhere from one to three questions before asking me to set up an appointment. Since I had no cash to hire a better attorney, I used what I did have—time. I compiled a list of every question I needed answered and telephoned every attorney in the yellow pages until I'd covered each, free of charge. I knew I would have to essentially defend myself and, sitting in the courtroom now, I'm glad I made that decision as I watch other incompetent or burnt-out public defenders allow their clients to be handed far steeper sentences than they deserve. It reminds me of how Tess' boyfriend was never punished for nearly killing her, yet she went to jail for driving his car.

The judge calls me to the stand and starts in on a series of questions for the trooper and me. Neither of us is sworn in. The judge examines my driving record despite the plaintiff's objection. Since it is out-of-state, the cop's lawyer argues its validity.

"So you've never had a run-in with the law," the judge says more than asks. "Do you have a job? One that pays, I mean?"

"Yes, your honor," I say. "I'm in graduate school full-time. Also,

I teach at two colleges. Also, since this experience, I've started teaching writing workshops to at-risk youth."

"That's enough," the judge interrupts. "You say she was cooperative during the arrest?"

"Yes, your honor," the trooper says.

"Let's reduce this reckless to speeding then," the judge says.

"I ask that you require this young lady to complete a driver's safety class," the cop's lawyer says.

"Is this agreeable?" the judge asks.

It's not agreeable to me, but my public defender shouts an affirmative. The judge tells me where to pick up my paperwork and, just like that, he moves onto the next case.

"I can't believe we won," my public defender says while walking back to our chairs to retrieve our belongings. "It's the first time I've won a case like this."

* * *

Now

I know the probability is low that Tess still works here with all the restaurants and bars in this world. Still, I dismiss mathematics and come here because I'm a writer and that's what most writers do. I've been thinking a lot about Tess lately. At the start of each semester at the community college, I'd scan my rosters for her name even though I knew ex-convicts couldn't get student loans from the government and Tess couldn't afford school without financial assistance. Still, I kept looking. I never came across her name. I wasn't even sure what her name was short for or even if it was short for anything. Then, I took a full-time job teaching at a four-year college out-of-state and I knew I'd never find her name on its rosters.

Tess is nowhere in sight. I picture her in a college classroom, wildly raising her hand, eager to answer any and all questions her professor asks. Then, I picture her back in prison. Since I won't let myself imagine her kids, bereft, motherless, I think instead of Tess being reunited with Desiree, teaching the woman how to read.

I want to ask the waitress for a refill on my water, but when I attempt to flag her down, I notice she's crying at the bar, her feet propped on the stool next to where she sits. The manager—I assume he's the manager because he's wearing a button-down shirt and tie that look inexpensive but still stand out here—rubs her back and neck. I decide they aren't dating and that this is probably some sort of sexual harassment. In this moment, it's almost as if she's Tess, as if she has the same types of problems with the same types of men. I'm in the process of splitting with my first bad boyfriend, too, one who's been manipulative and controlling, one who's taken advantage of knowing that I care and, so, I could understand a little better what Tess went through. I could see how my relationship could have turned darker, uglier, if I hadn't had the education to piece together what was happening and the self-confidence and options that came along with that education.

When I'd asked my boyfriend to help me find Tess, he declined. He couldn't imagine being seen in a chain restaurant. He also couldn't imagine my wanting to listen to and potentially help a person who I barely knew and whom he thought could do nothing for me in return. Suddenly, I see what he must be like out in the world and he is just like me that day in high school, observing my co-worker's kids at the bar and walking out when shit got too real.

"Does Tess work here?" I ask the waitress as she returns from her crying jag to check on me.

"Never heard of her," the waitress says. "I'm new here, though. Filling in for someone, I guess."

A song that sounds like "Send Me An Angel" blares and, even

though it isn't it, I pretend like it is. I think of Tess singing the way she had in our cell that morning, but her voice sounds better the way I chose to remember it.

I tear up thinking about her and where she might or might not be. Jailface isn't possible on the outside. What we each have to lose is much tougher than anything we could pretend to be and, when I think about all Tess has already lost, unfairly, a feeling of smallness almost swallows me up.

FREEDOM FROM EMMALINE

Linda Harris Sittig

"Welcome home! Today, you may call me Emmaline."

With those last six words, the universe tilted, and I slid into the chaotic world of my mother's mental illness.

I don't remember how she was dressed that day, although she most likely was wearing her Hepburn flats, pegged Capri pants, a freshly-pressed white blouse, and a scent of Charles of the Ritz perfume. Slender at 5'2", my mother's tousled chocolate brown curls belied the fact that she took the utmost care in her appearance, and so did Emmaline.

Let me be clear right from the beginning. This is not a story on split personalities, or multiple personalities, or even schizophrenia. It is a glimpse into an illness that robbed my mother of a normal life; an illness that permeated the lives of her children and inflicted invisible scars on each family member. Emmaline was merely a representation of the disease.

My single greatest terror growing up was that I would inherit my mother's "problem"—even though at the time, I could not name it, did not know what it was, or understand that my mother had no control over it. Throughout my teenage and young adult years, I consciously sought freedom from my mother's life, fearful that I could be carrying the same defect in my own genes.

The day she introduced herself as "Emmaline," my brother and I, at about six and ten, had just walked home from school. It had started out like any other ordinary day. We were growing up in a charming 1920s-era four-story house on a wide street sheltered by old oaks in a lovely refined neighborhood. By all accounts we appeared to be living the American dream. But our lives changed the day that Emmaline appeared and brought with her a delightful fantasy-like childhood game, which eventually deceived us all.

My father's work schedule as a Wall Street accountant often caused him to miss out on Emmaline's appearances and the magical moments of pure unadulterated fun that accompanied her. Our mother as Emmaline would announce that we could have Cheerios for dinner, stay up late, make a tent under the dining room table, and forgo a bath. It was rather like falling down the rabbit hole with Alice.

For the next year or so, Emmaline made sporadic visits—always unannounced. She would pop into our lives when we least expected it and leave when it suited her fancy. With Emmaline we would dine on cereal, play card games, and then stay up late and listen to my mother's wonderful stories of tiny fairies that wore purple bells on their shoes and came to dance in our bedrooms once we were fast asleep.

Emmaline would be all smiles and silliness, as compared to the sensible woman married to our father who typed out the P.T.A. newsletter, hosted bridge games with the neighbors, and arranged Cub Scout meetings at our house. Emmaline was never that mundane; life with her was filled with the glorious anticipation of what new excitement might be waiting just around the corner.

We never questioned when or why Emmaline appeared; we took her at face value and enjoyed her presence until she left.

Where she went, we never questioned either, and although we were disappointed at the void she always left behind, we knew she would eventually come back.

Of all the adventures with Emmaline, a summer picnic in a leafy park stands out the clearest—because of the laughter. The park was dense with maples and dogwoods and bisected by a wonderful babbling brook. Wooden picnic tables dotted the landscape, and the warm summer air dappled our faces. While my mother unpacked the lunch and my father smoked a cigarette by the brook, my brother and I decided to cross the water by stepping on the flat rocks that had created a serpentine path leading from one shore to the other.

Dressed in shorts, t-shirts, and summer sandals, we made it halfway across when a rock slick with wet leaves caused us to fall into the brook. Suddenly we found ourselves sitting in the rivulet while the cool water rushed over our legs. We broke out laughing and then looked back at the shore. My father was standing, shaking his head—dismayed perhaps that we had just ruined perfectly good shoes. But our mother was smiling in a way I had come to recognize as an Emmaline smile.

"Emmaline's coming to rescue you," she gleefully shouted and before our bewildered father even understood her mission, she pranced out onto the rocks and promptly slipped and fell into the water next to us. Sitting in the middle of the brook, she threw back her head and the peals of her laughter rang out through the canopy of trees. The three of us sat, splashing water on each other and laughing until we were filled to the brim with exhilaration.

"Mildred, get up and get the children out of there. They don't have any dry clothes and neither do you."

With that practical declaration, our laughter subsided, and Emmaline vanished before we reached the muddy bank.

After the incident in the park, my mother found a new friend that surpassed the need for Emmaline. My mother discovered vodka. Emmaline never returned and my mother slowly but steadily morphed into an alcoholic.

Once vodka joined the family, each year became more tumultuous and peppered with increasingly hostile family arguments that grew in magnitude as the sun journeyed across the sky. For my brother and me, our Emmaline years were abruptly replaced by our mother's growing Jekyll and Hyde personality. We watched her flirt with the mailman one minute and then shut the door and hurl caustic comments at us about our ineptitudes as her children

By the time I was in high school, being around my mother had became unbearable. Ordinary life had ceased to exist, and was replaced instead by vodka-fueled battles. I volunteered one night to help make dinner and my mother sneered at my pathetic naiveté concerning cooking and harped for twenty minutes on why no man would ever be interested in me due to my lack in culinary abilities. I retaliated by never cooking in her presence again. My social life was another thorn in her side. Once, just as I was ready to leave on a date, my mother suddenly demanded that I wear galoshes over my shoes or she would not allow me to leave the house. With my date by my side, I slid my feet into the horrid neon yellow boots and left with feelings of humiliation hanging all over me.

My brother and I blamed the vodka. We coped with her increasing erratic behavior by rarely inviting friends over to the house after school, because we never knew if she would be on one of her alcoholic tirades. In truth, she was a mean drunk. Never one to use any physical violence, she chose words for her weapons. While she fought to retain a sense of authority through her alcohol steeped verbal abuse, my father retreated into a cocoon of conflict avoidance.

My mother and I continued to argue about anything and everything. Dinner often ended with words so hurtful that I would actually choke on the food, push away from the table, and flee to my bedroom where I could lock the door and escape. My father would then trudge upstairs, knock, and tell me that my mother was having one of her 'difficult spells' and that I should ignore her.

But it's hard to ignore words that slice the soul.

Eventually, I chose a college ten hours away from home, and enrolled there in order to escape her.

Then one day in my late forties, I was reading a novel and came to a passage describing the dysfunctional family and manipulative mother of the story. I suddenly found it hard to breathe. There on the pages before me was a perfect description of my teenage years, word for word. *How could anyone else know these details?* I wondered in shock about the possibility that any other family had lived my same life. I read the diagnosis of the fictional mother—manic depressive disorder. At long last I understood that my mother's problem had been a form of mental illness, a disease that no one in the family had ever been willing to acknowledge, or discuss.

I read up on the disorder and quickly realized that Emmaline had been a part of her manic phases, and that when the depression side threatened to swallow her whole, she attempted to self-medicate with alcohol. No wonder being with Emmaline was magical; it gave my mother a chance to live joyously without any restrictions on proper behavior, even if only for an afternoon.

My father probably fell in love with her during one of her early manic episodes. She was upper middle class Philadelphia, tracing her ancestors back to one of the six original Swedes who settled the area forty years *before* William Penn arrived. Her D.A.R. lineage included a captain who loaned General George Washington the use of the family barn for a field hospital during the American Revolution, and there is even a street in Philadelphia named after her father's family. By all reports, she grew up with money and connections and was always considered to be the life of the party.

For my father, a first generation handsome British-American from a blue collar family, my mother must have been a dazzling creature who turned his world topsy-turvy as they attended parties and went out dancing and bar hopping together.

They had a whirlwind romance, married, and settled down to life in the West Village of Manhattan. Six months later came the attack on Pearl Harbor, my father was drafted into WWII, and they became separated for the next four years. By the time my father returned from Europe, they had to start their marriage over again.

After my brother and I were born, my father decided it would be a healthier way of life if he moved the family out to the suburbs. For my city-born, city-bred mother, I'm sure it was more of a death knell toward boredom.

Once they moved into the picturesque town in northern New Jersey, hints of my mother's mood disorder certainly surfaced. I guess my father either chose to ignore them, or believed she would get better on her own. Of course my mother never wished for this illness to consume her, and my father faithfully stayed with her until the bitter end.

By the time my mother died at age 61, alcohol had ravaged her body and a blood clot performed a mercy killing by lodging in her lung while she slept. She simply never woke up. But she finally did elude her demons.

For me at 27, the guilt about her death was overwhelming. If only I had tried harder, perhaps I could have saved her. The classic mark of a child of an alcoholic, I believed that in some insane way her problem was mine to solve. Even now as an adult, I still try to 'fix' family issues by attempting to soothe over any unpleasantness. It's a hard habit to break.

Manic depressive is the former name of what is now called bipolar disorder. Like other forms of mental illness, it tends to run in families and there is no definitive reason as to how it begins. Once diagnosed, patients normally begin a course of medications that help to stabilize the wild mood swings and they often stay on those mediations for life. Also like other forms of mental illness, there are varying degrees of severity. For our family, there were months of normal living in between her episodic moods.

My mother was not a monster. But the disease was, and none of us were equipped to slay the dragon. I do believe deep in my heart that she loved us and I still miss her every day. The good parts of her DNA passed straight through to my daughters—her creativity, her magnetic personality, and her flair for fashion. I often think how much my mother would have loved to know them.

What is my freedom? I have lived long enough without any 'Emmaline episodes' myself, that I am certain the disease has passed me by. I look into the mirror and see a confident woman who has been blessed in so many ways.

And never, not even once, has the face of Emmaline peered back at me.

Swing a Sparrow on a String

Ken Goldman

Angela opened her eyes to a new day, not knowing if it were morning. There were no windows in her room, and it could have been the middle of the afternoon, or even midnight. She heard no sounds except her own breathing, and when she awoke she inhaled and exhaled heavily, as if she had just completed a marathon race instead of having slept for hours. Perhaps she had slept for days. She had stopped wondering about time months ago. Now she simply slept for as long as she was able, then stayed awake for as long as was necessary.

She knew she would have to eat, that they would soon be coming with food, and had she felt stronger she might have spat it back at them as she had done when they first brought her here. But she had swallowed that rage a long time ago. Now Angela ate whatever morsels they gave her, and recently she had to restrain herself from thanking them. She feared the day might come when she would feel grateful that they had allowed her to live, when she might find herself smiling at them as if she understood and accepted the perfect correctness of her captivity.

She looked at herself in the small cracked mirror above the sink. Although her hair was stringy and unwashed, she remembered how golden it had shimmered in the sun. Her face was still quite pretty, and once she had heard one guard tell another he had never seen eyes quite that blue. The other whispered what a pity it was.

If only she had a piece of paper, a pen, even a crayon. Maybe this time she would show them that she could create something useful and lasting that mattered to them, something that in turn would make her matter. When Angela had first arrived, they had eagerly granted the request of the eighteen year old girl and waited to see what gifts her imagination might offer them.

She had succeeded only in producing a few formless scrawls that they said were not art, and some rhymeless gibberish that they told her was not poetry. They took away the paper, the pens, and the paint brushes.

Not long ago, the tall blond guard who wore the keys around his neck had asked her if she might like to sing. Any tune would do, he told her. "Please, oh please, let me try!" Angela had begged. The next day he brought to her room a small cassette recorder with a blank tape. "Perhaps we will find the song bird in you where we were unable to find the artist. Sing, and we promise to listen," he assured her.

For days Angela sang alone in her room, remembering what her mother had sung to her many years ago. *"Hush little baby, don't say a word. Mama's gonna buy you a mocking bird . . . "* A week later she handed the cassette to the man with the keys and simply said, "Please . . . " He stuffed the tape into his pocket and left without a word.

The next day the guard sat alongside her bed and informed her that he and the others had decided that she was no song bird. For a moment his words had sounded like an apology. She knew she would never see the tall guard again.

The wasted papers that Angela had filled with nonsense and the inarticulate squawks she had tried to pass off as music had convinced them that further efforts on their part would be foolish. From that day forward the guards who silently delivered her food seemed unwilling to even look at her.

Angela heard the key slip into the lock on the other side of the heavy door. She no longer pretended to be asleep when they came, because they did not care whether she were sleeping or awake. One of them always waited outside as the other entered. She heard the heavy jingle of keys and looked up. The keys were around the guard's neck.

"You," she said, but the word was only a statement of fact, not sparked with the warmth that accompanies the recognition of a familiar face. Once uttered, the word sounded idiotic.

"Yes," he answered, closing the door behind him. He did not look at her as he set the tray of food on the stand alongside her bed. She had expected no further conversation, and when he spoke again, his words startled her.

"They told me to say the other guard had caught a flu." He pulled up the small wooden chair and sat, although the chair was too small and he seemed not to know whether to fold his legs. "There is no flu. They wanted us to talk."

His statement was ludicrous. She had not had a conversation with him in months, and those few she remembered had been pitifully brief and one-sided. "I don't understand," she said as she selected a small bread crust on her tray. She had learned to keep her responses short, for the guards tired of her quickly.

"I'd like to know about God," he said as if this were meant as an answer. "Tell me how you feel about God. Tell me about your religion, your beliefs."

"I have no belief in God. I have no religion. Don't you have some sort of records about that?" She felt immediately sorry she had asked, but the guard ignored the question anyway. He fidgeted in the small chair.

"You're an atheist, then? Or an agnostic? You have opinions regarding God's existence, or the lack of it?" He sounded almost hopeful.

"I'm an apathist. I don't much think about it," she answered as she nibbled at the crust. She picked up a slab of egg yolk with her left hand, ignoring the silverware, leaned her head back, and dropped the yolk into her mouth.

Her response oddly pleased him, although he did not smile. "An apathist? That was a joke you just said. Admittedly, not a very good one, but it *was* a joke. Then you have a sense of humor. Tell me another joke."

Angela looked hard at the man, not certain about how earnest her guard's question was. "A joke? You mean like why did the chicken cross the road?" The absurdity of her question seemed to increase the guard's excitement.

"Yes! Yes! Tell me, why did the chicken cross the road?" There was anticipation in his voice as if he sincerely were interested in the chicken's intentions, and when he leaned toward Angela for her response, his face revealed the hint of a smile.

"Perhaps the chicken was an apathist," she said.

The guard's smile disappeared as quickly as if it were erased. "That isn't funny. I'm sorry, but that isn't funny at all." His tone became flat, expressionless. He sounded like a man keeping some kind of score. No points for humor. Sorry. Next category.

"Can we talk politics?" he asked.

"No."

"Sociology? Science? History? Law? Philosophy?" His questions now had become a formality, a check list to be completed, filed, and forgotten.

"No . . . No . . . No . . . No . . . " Although Angela could not remember ever having had a discussion this long during her stay here, she wanted this conversation to end. "Perhaps I could tell you why the philosopher crossed the road? No, I guess you're right. That wasn't very funny either. I suppose you'll be leaving now?"

Her question had anticipated his next words. The tall guard rose from the chair with difficulty, trying to maintain his dignity when he could not get up with his first attempt. "I have one more question for you, Angela," he said. He had never called her by her name before, and his doing so struck her as odd. He walked to the foot of her bed and turned toward her. "Do you know why you are here?" He asked this without malice or emotion, with only the desire to know her answer, as he had wanted to know about song birds and chickens.

"I'm here because you see me as a useless bird." Having said the words, she knew they had always been on her tongue waiting to be spoken.

"I beg your pardon?"

"You know, the sparrow who can no longer fly becomes useless to the other sparrows, a burden to them. I've broken my wing, isn't that right? And the flock has no further need of me."

"I'm impressed," the guard answered. "That is quite a creative analogy from one who knows so little of creativity." He sat on the edge of the bed and moved close to Angela as if to reveal a secret. Instead, he reached under the blanket and grabbed hold of her right hand, yanking it out from where she had kept it hidden. He held her arm straight up and the pain caused her to wince. "But this isn't exactly a broken wing, is it, Angela? It's a wilted arm, a useless limb. It is not pleasant to look at, it serves no function, and it belongs to you. It *is* you." The words came in furious bursts now, like machine-gun pellets, and he shook her withered limb as he spoke. "You see yourself as a wounded sparrow, do you? What happens if we take that sparrow and tie her leg to a string and swing her around in circles in a desperate attempt to make her fly? She struggles against hope to use her wings, her useless wings, and meanwhile we swing her around and around and around, wasting our energy, wasting our time, and in the end when we stop swinging her, she comes crashing down to earth anyway. Our time has been wasted, her hopes have been destroyed. What is the point? Why even bother?" He let go of her arm, allowing it to drop.

For a moment Angela stared at the shrunken arm as if it were a foreign thing that did not belong in the bed with her. She spoke without removing her eyes from it. "A sparrow who can no longer fly can sing. And if she can't sing, she can still feel, can still—"

"—Love?" the guard interrupted. "That's exactly right, Angela! We asked this sparrow to sing, and she could not! But we realized she may be capable of love . . . the kind of love that could only result in frustration for her. Because the real question is, is she capable of *being* loved? Do the words she writes encourage love? Does her beauty or intellect in any way inspire it? It is unlikely that anyone would even try to love her because of that hideous limb. Not that all physical impediments are repulsive. Perhaps if she were only blind . . . "

"Stop . . . Please, stop . . . " Angela pleaded. Her brief taste of defiance had made her want to gag.

"You want to cover your ears, don't you? You want to block out the words, make me go away, maybe you would even like to strike me," he continued. "But you can't do it, can you? That limb just lies there like a dead weight. Do you see my point?"

"I have my other arm . . . "

" . . . whose only function is to hide its companion. No, Angela, I'm sorry, but the time has come for us to stop swinging the sparrow's string." His anger slowly dissolved and he fell silent for a moment.

He attempted to hold her wilted hand in his, but she pulled it away. Instead he took her other hand. "But first I have something I want to show you, something you need to see." He sat on the bed and placed her fingers on his left leg below the knee. "Rub your hand along my leg, Angela. Does the calf feel peculiar to you? Congenital defect, they called it, like they called yours. The leg is gone, at least from the knee down. Amazing what they can do with prosthetics today. But, you see, I have my particular talents. I happen to be quite good at drawing people out, at enabling them to find a way to compensate for their physical shortcomings. And I can be quite decisive when called upon to make the kind of decisions that others would find distasteful. No one ever asked me to sing, or to fly. But when they came for me, I simply told them what I could do."

Angela struggled to pull her hand free as her anger rose inside her like hot bile. "But you also decide who is to be exterminated! You decide who the state no longer regards as useful! What gives you the right—"

"*This* gives me the right!" he shouted, his breath hot on her face as he tapped her hand on the hard wood of his prosthetic leg. "This has forced me to find my usefulness to others, just as your pathetic limb has forced you to admit that you have none. And I have no intention of relinquishing my usefulness by allowing you to continue your hollow existence. I refuse not to matter!"

The guard's renewed anger seemed to embarrass him, and he turned away from Angela. He ran his fingers through his blond hair in an attempt to collect himself, and when he again looked down at his leg, he noticed that Angela's hand was grasping it. Angela knew he had been unaware of her touch until he had looked. When his eyes locked with hers, her mouth curled in a bitter smile.

"I *feel* this," she said as she ran the tiny hand of the wilted arm along his wooden leg. "I feel this with both of my hands, even the one you call useless. Tell me what you feel when I touch you. Does this prosthetic device extend all the way to your heart?" Angela tapped on the artificial limb as if she were expecting a reflexive kick.

"A curious question," he answered. "You might have made a fine idealist if you had believed in God."

She moved close to his face and whispered, " . . . to get to the other side. That *is* why a chicken would cross the road, isn't it?"

He paused for a moment to look at her. "Such blue eyes," he said. "Such exquisitely beautiful blue eyes." He called for the guards to take her, and within moments three entered the room and another two waited by the doorway.

She presented no struggle and went quietly with them. She wondered as they walked if one of them would take her hand.

Hana Yori Dango

Dominic Cheverton

Hiroku looked down on the working town of Hikutsu Pass. A hundred people or so lived in the valley, in their small houses, tightly packed on the edge of Hima Lake. Each one was a rickety wood-topped shed, as could be found in any mining town. Each a far cry from the brown tiles and painted wooden architecture on the Meiji-owned Fukuwara Estate. Hiroku would often gaze from the vantage point on the path to the shrine, staring at the rich manse with the pristine gardens and ponds filled with koi, watching the patrolling guards on the outer wall. As he looked this time, he saw two guards laughing in a tower, training their rifles on one of the tired miners below. Hiroku's eyes narrowed angrily, his hand fell to his side and clutched the wooden swords, but he breathed a deep sigh and turned away as the guards laughed again and lowered their matchlocks.

"Hiroku. Hiroku. Are you ready to go?" His mother called, coming down the long steps into the trees. "We're all done with prayers, so we're heading back down to the restaurant." His baby sister, Sayumi, waved at a butterfly, giggling to herself, before brushing her long hair from her eyes. Hiroku glared at her.

"But, we're having noodle soup again," Hiroku complained,

pushing himself away from the wooden archway at the end of the steps. He ran a hand through his own hair, short and not nearly as full as his sister's.

"That's what your father is making though."

Hiroku puffed out his cheeks. "Well, I'm going to have an extra dumpling then. Noodle soup is so plain."

"Dumpling," Sayumi said, turning her face from the wind to smile at her brother.

"And don't let your father see you with those sticks. You know what he'll do."

He clutched his swords again. "I don't care what he does. Nobou-san didn't give up his swords. Father shouldn't have either."

"Hiroku." There was a reproachful tone in his mother's voice, but he wasn't saying anything he hadn't heard her say a dozen times before. "Come on." She put a soft hand on his cheek before turning.

Hiroku couldn't help but feel guilty when his mother did that. "When I run the restaurant, there will be dumplings for everyone; sweet and savoury, all day long." Hiroku thrust his chin upwards trying to look as grown up as possible.

* * *

A long trail of men and animals snaked down from the mountain, hauling iron ore to the foundry. Hiroku looked out from the hill one last time to the mountain peaks and the snow-covered Hikutsu Pass. The sun glared off Hima Lake, where something disturbed a group of ducks from the rushes. Squinting into the distance he caught sight of the train speeding around the lake like a slithering snake, with the great, dirty-grey dragon flying just above in the pure blue. He smiled and chased after his mother.

He caught them just before they reached the bridge at the bottom of the hill. Sayumi was waddling slowly on one side, gargling indecipherable words into the warm breeze, and his mother had collected a few sun-coloured flowers from the edge of the path. "There's a train coming," he called. "I saw it."

His mother heard and looked to either side of the bridge before speeding across, with Sayumi well in tow. Hiroku could hear the train already, the rolling of the wheels on the track and the heavy chug that drove the metal beast forward. He waited in the middle of the bridge, chewing his lip, the smallest touch of fear, as it drew closer. The rickety wood shook and rumbled beneath his feet as the train passed under the bridge, louder and stronger than a rushing waterfall. Hiroku stumbled a little, breathing in the smell of the dark smoke trail that bathed him completely; hot and thick, like breathing in a cloud of stormy thunder. He caught sight of his mother after the air cleared; she merely shook her head and pulled Sayumi along the path.

The wind jostled through the tall grass at the edge of the path, and rocked the boughs of the trees, ruffling the feathers of the sparrows that rested there. Hiroku brushed the hair back from his face, his skin cool in the summer sun after the heat of the train's smoke, and smiled at the simple beauty around him. That was the Samurai way, he had always thought, to live a simple, natural life. He touched his swords again before loosening the straps around his waist and depositing them behind a tree just off the path.

Nobou stood in front of the restaurant with two others Hiroku didn't know by name. They wore their tokin around their foreheads, marked for the Mitsuo clan, and strapped to their waists were their own swords, a pair of them each; so much better than Hiroku's stripped and smoothed sticks. Nobou fished around inside his clothes and rested his hands in his armpits. "You have a touch of Fukuwara in you after all, Resshin-san, you coward." Nobou's chest was barrelled out and his head high. His face was twisted, as though he were always chewing his cheek, and his balding head lolled to one side. "You may as well call yourself a Meiji and be done with it." He touched his swords, spitting into the dust of the thoroughfare and stormed away with the other two men close behind.

They disappeared around the corner of the last building as Hiroku's mother reached the restaurant. "Nobou-san was here, preaching against the Meiji," Hiroku's father was saying when he neared too. Sayumi was toddling across the floorboards into the corner, where her small toys were kept. "A representative is coming in today to speak with the Fukuwara, and he means to ambush him with Kiroku-san. I told him, no." He righted the stools on the floor, having been spilled in some disturbance, and sat. "Revenge for what they did to Kiroku-san's daughters, he says." He pushed his hand over his face as if brushing the anger away, "This man probably doesn't even know what happened here in the spring and he's going to be punished for it."

"He's Meiji, that's all they need to know."

Hiroku's father looked up from where he sat. "You think I should have gone? You think I should have beaten this man for the crimes of others?"

"The Meiji have ruined our way, Resshin."

"We rebelled, Yuki. We gave the Meiji their power."

"And you can take it away."

"No, we can't." His voice was raised slightly now, irritated. He stood sharply and began righting the rest of the restaurant.

Hiroku stepped inside, moving quickly to the back of the building without meeting his father's eye. The wooden frame wobbled slightly when he leant against it, but it was sturdy enough. The high mountains surrounding Hikutsu Pass protected the town from any strong wind, but the snowfall of many winters weighed heavily on their roofs; theirs was dipping in the middle like a fortunate fisherman's net.

He crouched in the corner playing with Sayumi's small, wooden horse. He trotted it across the floorboards and up her small, sausage leg, to her delighted squeals. "Dumpling," she said. His sister was a very talkative little girl, but that was the only word any of them could ever make out. She was oblivious to everything going on around them; to her, their parents never fought, their father never laid an angry hand on their mother, and she never said a word back to him about the Fukuwara. Hiroku envied his baby sister sometimes, so innocent and pure, like the buds of the Sakura yet to flower. She brushed her already flowered hair away from her face. Hiroku sighed.

"The Meiji have changed our world," Hiroku's father continued after a few moments. "I'm tired, Yuki, and there's no use fighting them anymore."

"What about your family's honour? What about having dignity and grace in death, like Nobou-san? You think he shames the Mitsuo? You think your father would be ashamed of him?" Resshin brought down his hand with such speed, it was as though it hadn't happened. Only, now his mother had tears in her eyes and she was holding her swiftly-reddening cheek.

"You do not mention that name to me." He rubbed the palm of his hand before moving behind the screen at the back of the room.

"At least Fukuwara had honour."

He was out from behind the screen in an instant and charging across the restaurant floor. Yuki had fear in her eyes and stumbled backwards, tripping to fall when she reached the small ledge by the thoroughfare. "Stop, Hiroku. Stay back," he shouted when Hiroku made to help her. He stopped on the spot and retreated, staring angrily at his father.

"My father was the first to sell arms to the Meiji," Resshin continued. "He ordered our rifles to Hima. I wanted nothing to do

113

with it, but honour forced my hand." There were tears in his eyes as he retreated to sit on the nearest stool and took a few deep breaths. "It's so much easier than with a katana, Yuki. So much quicker. You don't have to watch the light fade in their eyes. You don't have to see the last blossom of their lives falling, failing. There is no honour, no respect, in firing a lead ball through a man's back as he flees." His words stuttered more and more.

Yuki walked to her husband, brushing the dust from her clothes, and knelt beside him, resting a hand on his leg.

"It's not cowardice, Yuki. I want the Meiji brought down as much as Nobou-san or any of the Mitsuo. But our way is dying. Our way is the fading light in the eyes and the Meiji are the rifles. None of them can see that the Meiji have already won. The Samurai are dead." He spared a brief glance for his own son. Hiroku glared back. "We have to be practical now, we have to look after our families, not our way of life. That's what matters."

Hiroku was still stuck on the spot. He wanted to scream at his father, *You're wrong. That's not what matters; honour and our way of life is what's important.* But he knew what would happen if he did. So he seethed quietly and retreated to his sister's corner of ignorance.

* * *

"Fukuwara Resshin-san?" Hiroku looked back to see the four men at the entrance. Three were tall and dressed in tight suits of the Meiji, black and yellow, each had identical trimmed moustaches and narrowed, beady eyes peering from beneath their flat-topped hats. Long, thin swords hung at their waists and rifles over their shoulders. The fourth man was short and squat, with similar black attire only his hat sat perfectly rounded on his head.

"Yes?"

"I've never been to Hikutsu Pass before, but I'm told that this is the best place to get some refreshment." It was the small man who was speaking, an airy, lisping voice.

"Yes. Yes of course, but I'm sure there is tea on the Fukuwara Estate . . . " He paused, waiting for the man to introduce himself by name.

"Okasa."

"Okasa-san." Hiroku's father stood, dutifully inviting them into the restaurant.

"Mr. Okasa, please, Resshin-san." The small man smiled. "I'm sure they do, but then I would miss out on all of this rural charm, wouldn't I?" He smiled again, passing into the restaurant, tipping his hat just a little, then setting it on the table as he sat. The three tall men remained outside, perfectly on guard. Hiroku thought of Nobou and his threat to beat the man from the government. But he couldn't stop staring at the rifles on the men's shoulders. He'd never been so close to one before, taller than he was and as thin as a sword. He half wondered if they would let him hold it, but he knew better than to ask. He also knew they were far more dangerous than the swords he had held a hundred times. If Nobou arrived looking for trouble Hiroku was in no doubt who would win the fight. Maybe his father was right, maybe it was no use fighting.

Hiroku's hands found the inside of his clothes, slipping into his armpits, and he chewed on his lip, shuffling where he stood. The Samurai may have been dying and the fight lost, but all they taught couldn't be wrong in any world. Honour, respect, family.

"Father, I'll make the tea for Mr. Okasa." Hiroku stepped behind the screen as the men continued to talk. The water was already boiling and a pan of soup was cooling to one side. Hiroku poured the tea and watched as the steam rose like a ghostly tree. He saw the cloth package stuffed away in the rafters of the roof, swords, retired and disused. Kept as a reminder of what the world was; of what he was, Hiroku had heard his father say.

Sayumi pulled at his leg and garbled a handful of words at him, followed by "Dumpling." She smiled, poking her small teeth over her lips, her other hand still clutching to the small wooden horse.

"Hiroku." His father sounded impatient. "The tea."

He rubbed his little sister on the top of the head and rounded the screen, brushing a hand through his hair. His mother was busy tidying the rest of the furniture, her clothes were straightened and she looked as dutiful a wife as she did every day, but Hiroku thought he could see the hand print on her cheek. She left, moving into the backroom where they all slept, sliding the door closed behind her. Hiroku placed the tea on the table before Mr. Okasa, who bowed slightly in thanks and returned to the quiet conversation with Hiroku's father, who was sat opposite.

"I don't think your father would have tea as nice as this," Mr. Okasa said, sipping at the small cup.

Resshin poured himself a cup and joined the government man. "I'm sure the Estate has better tea, from Kyoto even." Hiroku could tell his father was irked at the mention of the Fukuwara. He wondered if he would slap Mr. Okasa as well, but he ventured a polite smile instead.

"On the contrary, there is something greatly refreshing about the rustic, don't you think?" The small man pressed down his moustache with a thumb and forefinger, repositioning his hat on the table.

"I wouldn't know, Mr. Okasa, I have only been to the city once."

"Ah, yes. Tokugawa's fall, no? I was there as well, you know. I never saw the man himself, but I was among the crowd." He shifted on his stool and smiled at Hiroku's father, who nodded.

"Would you like some soup, Mr. Okasa? I have some noodle

soup ready, and dumplings too."

"That would be delightful, I'm sure, Resshin-san."

"Hiroku." His father ordered with a sharp nod, before returning his attention to his guest. "So, what business do you have with the Fukuwara today?"

Hiroku bowed to them both, before eying the three guards still standing vigilant outside. He returned behind the screen and replaced the pan of soup on the flames. Sayumi was still there, sat on her bottom with her hands stretched out to grab her feet; she lost balance and rolled to her back, still clutching her toes. Her head smacked the wooden floorboards and she stared at Hiroku with a mixture of anger and confused tears. "Well, what do you expect?" He crouched by her side and righted her, kissing her on the top of the head and bringing her into a hug to stop the tears. She tried another few words at him before settling on the only one she could pronounce. "Dumpling. Dumpling."

Hiroku smiled at her and poured the re-boiled soup into a bowl. He pulled a dumpling from another bowl and took a bite, smiled and blew the tower of steam away from the soup before carrying it back out to Mr. Okasa, with a fresh dumpling. Mr. Okasa thanked him with a bow. "I trust you understand."

"Of course, I didn't mean to pry." Hiroku's father bowed apologetically, respectfully.

Mr. Okasa smiled and blew on his soup. "There are no illusions or secrets about the importance of the iron from Hikutsu Pass, Resshin-san."

Yuki slid the backroom door open again and padded in quietly; her hair was freshly brushed and tied. She gave Hiroku a quick, loving smile, sparing just a wary glance to all of the men in sight. Sayumi appeared from behind the screen, waddling like a duck with a smile just as large as one as well. She was waving her wooden horse in one hand and holding onto the building's central, wooden frame for support.

Everything then seemed to happen in a single instant. His mother screamed and there were shouts from outside the restaurant. Stools scrapped backwards and hit the floor as the men stood, adding their own confused voices to the discord. Hiroku turned, keeping his sister behind him, just in time to see the first of the guards hit the dusty thoroughfare; an arrow was buried almost to the fletching at the collar of his shirt. The other two were already raising their rifles. They fired with a burst of sunlight and a puff of black smoke. Hiroku thought for the briefest of moments that the train was driving right through the restaurant. His ears hurt and everything was silent but for the pitched ringing; he felt his mother grab for him and pull him towards the screen at the back.

His arm slipped away; she was already returning. Mr. Okasa lingered in safety by the restaurant's entrance, peering around the wooden wall at what was going on. Hiroku's father was standing by him, just outside; he was shouting something along the thoroughfare; muffled voices shouted a reply. The swift swords of the two remaining guards banged loosely, uselessly, at their hips and they still fretted about their rifles, as slow as a falling blossom on a breathless day; it wasn't made any easier by their dying friend clawing at their legs with a bloodied hand.

Hiroku's arm was grabbed again, stronger this time. Back behind the screen his mother pulled him, but he couldn't take his eyes from the scene. A figure launched itself through the air at one of the guards, his glinting tanto aimed for the throat; it didn't miss and the dusty yellow was inked a dark red. The final Meiji soldier raised his rifle at Nobuo. Hiroku heard his mother scream again, a frantic word, but his ears were still ringing, and it was hard to make out. Nobuo readied himself instantly after the last kill and charged. Hiroku could see the white in the eyes beneath the flat topped hat and the trembling half raised barrel of the rifle.

The ringing quieted, and Hiroku heard everything then. He heard the final breaths bubbling from the first felled guard. He heard voices further off in the village and the scraping of feet in the dust outside. He even thought he heard the whistle of the train leaving the station of Hikutsu Pass, drowned out by Nobuo's bear-like roar.

"Resshin-san, come back," Mr. Okasa yelled when Hiroku's father charged towards Nobuo. Hiroku didn't look anywhere else.

"Sayumi," his mother screamed.

He couldn't help but turn away then.

Sayumi had waddled off in tears, reaching her arms for her corner, her own little world; her wooden horse had been forgotten on the floor.

There was a yell of pain from outside as the guard hit the floor and a third deafening crack of thunder from the rifle. The middle of Sayumi's body jolted horribly to one side, leaving her feet and head where they were. For an instant it seemed as though she had stumbled in her waddling walk, but she hit the floor before Hiroku could reach her. He slid across the floorboards on his knees and scooped her into his arms. Most of her clothes had been stained red and her hands were dark and sticky, but her face was only marked by the tracks of tears. Hiroku brushed them from her cheeks with a thumb, even as his own fell. She looked just as she always did. Dimples pricked themselves in her cheeks and there was a soft smile in her eyes, only her eyes blinked slowly now, as if she were tired and ready for sleep after a long day of playing.

He brushed the hair from her forehead and kissed her.

Her small hand reached up and her fingers brushed the edge of his nose; ever so softly she spoke, "Dumpling." She smiled a small smile and her eyes, not so bright and innocent now, faded gently to a dull, tear-glistened brown.

Hiroku turned, still holding her. His mother was racing over and Nobuo was standing over his defeated enemy, until Resshin tackled him to the floor. Mr. Okasa was crouching behind the wall in the corner opposite Hiroku. His round, black hat rolled on the floor by the table where he had sat; it was smothered in spilled soup and a patch of white flour surrounded the red meat stain from the crushed dumpling.

FIREDANCER

Lyn McConchie

"Witch, witch! Firebringer!"

The yells came first, then the stone. The girl dodged, but the second struck hard. She'd come down from the mountains to trade the last of her father's furs for flour, salt, and perhaps a little tea or coffee. Another stone flew past and she hurried her steps. She reached the trading post, made her trade, and threw the sack over her shoulder, slipping away by the back door.

"Witch, yah! Witch!"

They'd found her again. A stone grazed her cheek, bringing blood. The girl had a sudden savage impulse to turn on them. She fought her anger, but the spark burned. She was no different to them. The Olsens could make the crops grow. Everyone admired the way their corn and other crops were always better than anyone's. The dark-eyed Branlys made music to entrance. No one called *them* witches and threw stones.

But she . . . Her name was Janda Shellin, and at this time and place she was just fourteen. She moved with a light, swirling grace, and her fine-boned face was attractive with high cheekbones and storm-gray eyes. She was an odd mixture of races. Her mother had been

Basque, that different secretive people whose origins even now, are uncertain.

Her father had called himself Martin Summer in jest. Western men sometimes asked if a name was a man's "Summer" or "Winter" name, indicating the possibility he'd changed it as he came West. Martin Summer *had* done so and taken the new name half joking. Once he'd carried another, but it told his homeland too clearly to those who knew. That was a place of rock isles and strange stories. The men from there were looked at sideways by the people of mainland Britain. Martin would rather it didn't happen here.

He'd wed an orphan girl and took her West with him to live in the mountains, away from other settlers and the hotter, more settled lowlands. She was woods-crafty, knowing the mountains and they were happy. The Comanche came rarely and the Apache passed through but traded with a man who knew both tongues and traded honestly. At least, it was so for Martin Summer.

Janda was born in solitude and trained in the ways of survival. Her mother had talked to her, taught her daughter to read and write, told her the maxims of her people and their stories, their beliefs. Her father had told her his and added his own knowledge of the ways of the animals here. Of hunting, trapping, and their associated arts. Her mother had died of a fever when Janda was twelve, and the girl still missed her. Her father had died almost a year ago. He'd been ill too. A fever caught from heaven only knows where. Ignored until it struck so hard even her casual father had to take to his bed.

He'd been asleep when Enright turned up. Janda had gone out to welcome the old prospector. Hearing her voice talking to someone, Martin Summer had tried to rise. He'd fallen back in a faint, but the jolt of his movements had knocked the lamp from his bedside. It broke, flaming oil running across the old wood. By the time Janda and Enright realized the cabin was on fire, the inside was already an inferno. Janda had not hesitated; she run into the roaring flames, dragging Martin from his bed and out into the open. Then she'd tended him as much of what they'd owned was reduced to ashes.

Enright had gaped as she emerged from the fire. Why, she wasn't even scorched. Martin had needed hot food, a fire and without thinking, Janda reached for a length of flaming wood. Her fingers closed over the burning portion, but she was too worried over her father to take notice. Nor did she see the old man shy back from her, his eyes widening. She cared for her father all that night. He died with the sunrise, and Enright helped her dig the grave. His subsequent farewells were brief and uneasy. When next she came down the mountains to trade alone, she found the fruits of his chatter.

Janda sighed bitterly. It hadn't helped that it had been a long, hot, very dry summer after that. The prairie fires had come more often from the heat lightning. Two farms had been burned out, their inhabitants escaping with no more than their wagon and horses and what they could carry. They'd remembered old Enright's talk, and from that the thing had spread. Most of the adults probably no more than half-believed it for the excitement. But their children made her rare visits down the mountains a misery.

She paused in the steep ascent to look back. Heat lightening danced on the plains. She reached the cave near the ruins of the cabin and dropped her sack. Her horse nickered to her, and Janda smiled. She entered her cave, laying away the various goods she brought back. At least she now had ammunition for her father's guns. Janda prepared food and ate as she considered. She could go back to the lowlands permanently and find work as a servant, or a waitress. She could stay here and hunt as her father had done. There were no relatives to whom she could turn. Anywhere she went she would be alone.

She finished her food, banked the fire and slept—to be awakened by the clatter of hooves. Janda awoke swiftly, sliding to the mouth of her cave, the primed and loaded gun ready in one hand. Enright's powerful black mule appeared, the old man urging her on. The mule stopped by the cave and Enright leaned over, his eyes guilty.

"I'm right sorry, girl. 'S all my fault. I'm an old fool who talks too much, and I sure done it this time. Thet was the Olsen kid cut your face with a stone yesterday, wasn't it? Well, las' night lightening set their cabin afire. They all got out but the kid. He burned. They're coming fer you, girl. They'll bury the kid an' then they'll be acomin' to burn you the way Joey Olsen burned. I'm sorry, girl, it's all my fault, so I come to warn you."

Janda thought quickly. Yes, they'd wait to bury the boy, then they'd have a few drinks. By that time it would be dark. They'd wait for daylight, but then they'd ride. If she left in the next hour or two, she'd have a good start. Already the Comanche were beginning to attack the farmers. In turn the settlers stayed away from the inner tribal lands. If Janda followed the mountain trails around back of the lower land, she'd end up behind Comanche territory where the settlers would hesitate to follow. If she could make them lose the trail before then, they wouldn't even be sure where she'd gone. She was packing her gear even as her mind leapt from plan to plan. Enright sat on his mule, watching.

"I sure am sorry, girl. It was jest a tale fer the evenings. I didn't mean you no harm. Yer pa was allus a good friend to me."

Janda nodded. "I know. There's some things I can't take. Why don't you pack them on the mule? It'd be a shame to see them wasted." She glanced at him. "An' I noticed Daisy's chipped a hoof. Let me clean that up while you pack. Just to show you there's no hard feelings."

She dug out the rasp and set to work while the old man scuttled about collecting her discards. Janda hid a dangerous smile. None of that stupid bunch down there were hunters. Her hands worked busily first on one hoof, then on the others. Enright would have noticed, but he was too busy scavenging. When she was done, she turned to helping the old man load the patient mule. She waved him away down the trail.

"I don't blame you for anything, but you'd best take the old trail along the ridge an' around. The ones who's coming might get nasty if they think you warned me."

He nodded and rode off, the scavenged gear clanking slightly as he went. Janda looked after him. Like hell, she didn't blame him. Her father had been Enright's friend. Martin had done the old drunkard many favors over the years, and her mother had fed him often. As a return for food and kindness, he'd talked about Janda until the settlers thought her the devil's own daughter. Now she'd be driven out of the only home she'd known just because the idiot liked to gossip.

She smiled again. He hadn't seen what she was doing to Daisy's feet. But with file and rasp she'd given them the look of shod hooves. It wouldn't last, just a day or so's riding, but the mule was heavily loaded and a large animal. Janda would brush over the trail she and Buck made when they left. With good fortune the lynch party would follow Daisy and Enright. She'd sent him the long way home, but it could easily be taken for an attempt to reach the road North. If the mob caught up with Enright, they'd likely hang him in frustration at losing her. Too bad!

She looked about the cave. Everything she could use was loaded on her mount. Janda nodded to herself as she walked off, leading the dun. Once she had him well away, she returned to cover their tracks. Back with him again she continued to walk. She had time; the fresher he was, the better he'd travel later if she needed to ride hard.

She never did have that need. As she swung down the faint trail around the back of the plains a day later, old Enright was just dying.

The lynch party had followed his trail in error. Seen his scavengings once they caught up. Then hung him in a rage at being tricked and in the belief he'd done so deliberately. After that, they returned muttering to their homes.

Janda plodded on. For the next year she lived solitary, trapping and hunting until her more civilized supplies ran out. She sometimes saw riders but avoided them all. Finally, she was so hungered for salt, sugar, and a good cup of strong tea that she ventured down from her hideout. On Buck she carried a small bundle of skins, all of them cured and tanned superbly. To the South there was a trading post. If she could make it there safely, make her trade, she would have supplies for a year, maybe two if she was very frugal. She made it to the post without difficulty.

But the sight of a girl with skins of that quality, and the amount she was paid for them, set men noticing. Two followed. Dregs from some city fetched up out West, and she lost them easily enough, but it made her twitchy. After that she hid from humanity like one of the beasts she hunted. A year passed, and another. She had to ride to the post again. By now Janda was almost eighteen. Her gift had matured and been refined in the long years of solitude.

She could call fire to burn sticks no matter how wet the wood. She could walk casually through the blaze of a grass fire unharmed. She'd found that did not apply to her clothing, although worked deerskins burned less readily. And she could work the lightening. She'd found that out the second year of her exile. A storm had brewed, and lightening had begun to strike about her camp. Somehow she found she was able to tell where each blow would fall. She saw then where the next would land and without thinking—she acted. Pulled aside from her horse, the lightning struck further away as Janda stared at her achievement, sitting down abruptly.

All that summer she worked at training her new and older abilities. It was something to do, and it made her feel safe. The next trip to the far trading post was uneventful. In her buckskins and with her hair hidden, Janda looked no more than another young lad. The Comanche were out, and no man was interested in some unknown boy. Only the store-keeper might have said different, and he was a taciturn man who said little at any time.

But in the moonlit night after her return to her temporary home, other things moved. The Comanche were shifting camp, and in the high hills, a storm brewed. An end-of-summer storm which would strike with a savagery peculiar to that season. It struck mid-morning while all were abroad. In the new Comanche camp, the adults were busy. Children wandered; some had left for a patch of berry bushes below a bluff. Unknowing of the camp's shift, Janda rode quietly down a narrow trail. It wound along a bluff and up into the high country where she would be safe once more.

The storm came swiftly and in silence. But she had seen and there was cover. A good deep cave which would take both her and her mount. She led Buck in and unsaddled him. He was too sensible to leave and stood three-legged, half-asleep as they waited. The storm struck in a bolt of lightning which crashed into bushes below the cave. It had been a long, dry summer. The impact was answered with a wall of flame. In seconds, the outer circle of bushes was alight and the fire spreading. From behind the flames came screams of childish terror.

The wind blew lightly away from Janda so that at first she heard nothing. Not so the Comanche. A mother was already searching for her daughter. She came running. Minutes after that, many of the camp had come in answer to her cries, but there was little they could do. The fire roared hungrily, catching hold of other dry brush—and behind that wall of fire, three children cowered and shrieked for aid. It was the commotion that finally caught Janda's ears. She crawled from the cave to look cautiously over the edge of the low bluff. The brush had lit in a circle, and as she watched, the center space that had still been clear narrowed further in a new gout of flame.

The children crowded together too terrified to scream now, their faces lifted to the sky. She could hear the oldest boy raise a quavering chant as he stood, arms around a girl and a smaller boy. Janda had heard that chant once. The child sang their death song as befitted a warrior. She looked at them then. The oldest no more than ten, the girl perhaps two years younger, the smallest boy only a toddler. The two oldest had pushed him between them, shielding him from flying sparks with their own bodies. But in a few minutes, the fires would close in. Nothing would shield him then, nor those who tried to do so. The chant rose up, firming as the boy drew strength from it.

Above them, Janda looked down on three children who would die a terrible death. She saw how, in the circle outside the fire, women wept. One tried to run into the flames, others held her back. Drawn as if by destiny Janda stood, slowly she walked down the steep slope. The fire raged, but it obeyed when she reached it, parting to let her through. Beyond the fires, the Comanche fell silent, watching. From their medicine man, there came a soft whisper.

"Fire Dancer!"

Janda stepped into the tiny space still left clear of the flames. The children ran to her as she reached out her hands.

"Come with me," she said softly in their tongue. "Keep close, hold your heads down as near to me as you can." She gathered them in. As she turned, a puff of wind came. With a rush, the fire closed in on the tiny group. "Take a deep breath and hold it," Janda ordered.

They obeyed as she marched forward. The heat was stifling, the air sucked away by the fire, but safety was no more than ten steps away. Their clothing wisped into ash, but the children's contact with Janda held back the flames from their bodies. They walked from the fire unhurt still clutching at her waist and arms with all their strength. Mothers swooped, crying, weeping with joy and fear.

The old medicine man walked forward, his eyes searching the girl's face. With the wisdom both of his age and his power, he read much. His hands waved back any who would have approached.

"Bring the white buffalo-skin robe from my tent for the Fire Dancer. Let her come to us in honor. Let food be prepared that we may feast her." He took Janda's hand. "Those of your blood are dead and you walk alone. Walk a little way with us. Ahead your path forks. Learn your choices that you may make them truly."

Drawn by the kindness in his voice and eyes, she followed. A medicine robe was placed about her shoulders. Later she sat by a camp fire and ate with her new friends. And somehow, without any definite decision made, she stayed. From Talks With Mountains she learned of her gift. It was not unknown to the Nemunah, the Comanche. Once, many generations ago, a medicine woman had the gift and the people had lived well and in greater safety because of it.

"There is an entrance to the land of the Gone-Before Ones," Talks With Mountains told her late one night. "It is empty and wide. All of the animals we have dwell there, all but the horse. Long ago, she who was Fire Dancer before you could open a path for us to that land. In bad winters, we sometimes stayed there for moons until the time of hunger was over because there the seasons are the opposite to those here. Yet always we returned. Our hearts cried for this land."

"How did she open the gate?"

"With the lightning. For a Fire Dancer who can call the lightning there is great power within that strike."

Janda studied him. "I can't call it."

"Not yet. To learn takes many years, but I can teach, Fire Dancer." His hand came out to grip her arm, "If you will learn?"

Janda sat in silence, Talks With Mountains letting her be to think. She remembered the hatred of the settlers. She was different, her gift a threat. She'd done nothing, never tried to hurt them. Just being different had been enough. They'd come riding in the end to murder her for being born with a gift they didn't have, had never seen before. In a daughter of two races, abilities had melded, shifted to something new to her lines. The Comanche had accepted her. To them the gift was a known thing and valuable to the people. Expressions passed over her face, grief, anger, joy, then slowly her face settled into lines of decision. She stirred as her eyes met those of her teacher.

"I will learn all you will teach me. My people cast me out for my gift. Yours have taken me into their tents. Your people shall be mine from now on. When do I begin to learn?"

Talks With Mountains smiled. "Tomorrow, after you have rested. Yet it will not be I who teaches you always. I can show you the path, tell you of the signs by which you travel. You alone can walk that road, Fire Dancer. Yet I believe you will walk it well. Go now and sleep."

She went to her blankets, but it was some time before she slept. Had she made the right decision? She slept then and with the morning came a cleared mind. This was her right choice, her true path.

The years passed as she walked the paths of learning. She learned to light the wettest stack of wood with a flick of her mind. Those first winters the people valued her greatly for that ability alone. Later she learned to divert all of the lightning in a storm away as if she held an umbrella over the camp. That saved the lives of many when in her tenth year in the camp, a storm struck at the area in which they cowered. Fifteen years after her arrival, she mastered the last teachings. Lightning came at her call, and she could control the strikes, directing them as she wished.

But outside her clan, time had not stood still. The white man had swarmed into Comanche lands in their hundreds at first, then in their thousands. The Comanche killed until the grass ran red, but still the settlers came, and there were always fewer of the people with each winter. Talks With Mountains had foreseen much. He and the Chief had drawn their people back, far into the mountains. They were a small clan within the larger Nemunah. Only thirty families and they could ill afford to lose lives.

Now, from the mountains, the warriors rode out to fight, but those who did not fight remained safe. Yet already settlers were moving towards the higher lands. Talks With Mountains waited, his dreams had spoken. At last his adopted daughter mastered the final facets of her gift. After the first Spring storm, she came to him laughing in pride.

"Did you see? I did it, I called the lightning. Then I made it strike at the cliff there."

"You did indeed, Fire Dancer. Now there is one more thing to learn. One more thing you must be able to do."

Janda smiled. "I know. Open the road of the Gone-Before Ones. Will it be a hard thing to learn?"

He shook his head. "No, but you must be further trained as a warrior. You command your mind, your gift. You must learn now to command your body past exhaustion. It must obey you though it die in the doing of your will. It will take all spring and much of the summer for this teaching."

"I will learn it," Janda said quietly. "Then in the fall, I will open the road for our people."

"It is well, daughter in power."

And it was. Janda endured and learned. She grew lean and hard, and still she worked with her gift until it answered even as she thought.

The children she had saved were adults. The men brought meat to her tent, the women brought worked deerskins as gifts. Janda lived alone, but her tent was always pitched beside that of Talks With Mountains. As he aged, she took over more and more of his duties for the tribe. By the end of that summer, she was ready.

"There is a special place. We must go there taking certain things." He lifted a doeskin pack. "I have all we shall need, Fire Dancer. Are you ready?"

She nodded. They rode away, the people watching in prayerful silence. A day later they returned, Janda drooping on her mount's back, in her exhaustion only half aware that they were home again. She was helped down, fed, cared for and laid on her blankets to sleep. Beside her Talks With Mountains sat chanting softly. Triumph! The road had opened to the Fire Dancer's demand. Better still, she had not only lived, she was simply exhausted. In two or three days, once she regained her strength, she could open the road again if she wished.

In a week, they left for the medicine place a second time, and this time Janda was able to open the road and walk away on her own feet. Both started their return rejoicing. They reached the camp to find it in turmoil.

"What is this?" Talks With Mountains' voice was suddenly fearful. Had his dreams come true so soon?

It was the Chief who answered, his tones sad. "Word has come from others of the People. The white men gather in great numbers with guns to attack us. If we go North or South, the Apache will drive us back. Those lands are theirs. If we go deeper into the wild lands, there is less food, the hunting is poorer. Where shall we go, what shall we do? Our tribe is less with each spring. Must we be as the snows that vanish with summer."

Talks With Mountains waited. Beside him Janda stirred, then

132

she walked forward to turn and look at her people. "I came to you as a stranger and you gave me honor. My own kind cast me out. Now they will move against you as they would have killed me—because I am different. Talks With Mountains taught me to cherish that difference and to use it. I had one last lesson to learn. It is learned. Listen to my father in heart."

The old man's voice was clear as he gave orders. The people ran to obey. Young boys fanned out on fast ponies to watch the trails. Women packed, warriors gathered the horse herd. Overhead, a great storm threatened. To the South there was another where men rode, carrying guns to a killing. One by one the scouts returned with word. The camp packed. Two days and a night. The men who hunted were almost to the camp. The Chief mounted, signaled and rode out as the people followed in grieving silence, wrapped in the chill winds of fall. They were leaving their land forever, yet it was better to leave than to die, and for their children's children, the new land would be their heart.

Ahead in the medicine place, Janda waited with her father in power. About him he wore a long woolen blanket so that only his head and hands showed. When all were assembled, she walked towards the rocks. Before them was a small grassy clearing. Janda faced the clearing and opened her gift. Above her the storm came, bellowing its fury. In the abandoned camp a day's ride away, men sought angrily for the trail. The storm howled power, Janda lifted her hands, and the lightning came, flaming about her, striking closer and closer as she seized it with her gift. She lifted her head, her fingers thrust out, hands spread, calling with all she was.

The storm rose to madness and then—as the lightning flared to crash down into the clearing—there was a flowing, a warping of the air, as a road opened into a land that was soft with a coming spring. The Chief swung onto his pony and led the people forward. Last came Janda, but Talks With Mountains waited still within the clearing. She turned.

"Come quickly, the door will close."

His smile was quietly accepting. "I cannot, daughter in power. For so many to cross when none plan to return there must be a price. Power gathers against you. When the road shuts, it will strike. But if I remain here, it is I who will die. The people will be free in their land and you shall walk with them."

Janda stared, tears welling in her eyes. "No!"

"Yes." He was adamant. "For all great power there is a payment to be made. I make it willingly. I am old and tired and my gifts fail me. You are young, and those you have chosen as your people will need you in the days to come. The Great Spirit rides with you, Fire Dancer. Let the road close."

She looked into his spirit as he had taught her. It was true, all of it. She did not see what he still withheld. Long ago in the medicine dreams of his youth, he had seen the way this would be. He had seen the danger, the destruction of his people. He had seen the one who would come. If she were made welcome, trained in power, taught to love the people, then she would be their gate to freedom. At first that was all she had been to him despite his kindness. But over time he had come to care. Once, he had planned to let her die when the road shut. Now he had chosen again, knowing in his heart that it was right.

Into his last words he put the dregs of his waning power. "Fire Dancer. You are Fire Dancer of the Nemunah. Go into the land and make it your own."

Janda bowed her head. Slowly she drew her mount backwards from the clearing. Step by step as she cleared the door she had created. Talks With Mountains took a rolled blanket from his pony, sending the mare after the others with a quick slap. He laid the soft length of wool out on the ground, stripped the other blanket from about his body as Janda gasped. Beneath the wool, he wore the sacred white buffalo-skin clothing. Swiftly he bound eagle feathers about his head, placed bracelets and necklaces of rattlesnake rattles on his neck, wrists and ankles. Then he lay down and began the death chant.

Behind Janda the tribe was moving away; this was medicine business. She remained waiting, watching. Her skin crawled as power rose again. The chant was done. Across the clearing, gray eyes met black ones in love and farewell. Lightning lit the clearing again and again to blue-white fury and—the road closed. Fire Dancer, medicine woman of the Comanche clan, claimed now and forever as her own, sat a moment before she turned to follow her people. Later those who hunted them came to the clearing. They found nothing there, only fire-scarred rocks and a drift of black ash whirling lightly on the chill wind.

Caterpillar Flu

Val Muller

Standing at the podium, Principal Elders opened a file folder. Around him, the auditorium seats creaked.

"Are there any other questions before we begin?" he asked.

The room was quiet. All eyes flew to the clock on the wall. Everyone knew the protocol. Fewer questions meant a faster staff meeting. And then they could all go home.

"Well, then. Before we move on to discuss new state standards, I wanted to talk about flu season."

The auditorium buzzed.

Principal Elders adjusted his jacket and pulled his tie tight against his neck. Then he held up a hand to silence his staff. They quieted. He had trained them well. "The nurse has left a memo in each of your mailboxes outlining proper protocol for containing the H3N7 flu. A few of you have started wearing the masks. This is fine—and the school board is considering making it policy." His eyes searched each row, looking for signs of obedience. Familiar nods greeted him. Some teachers even took notes. He nodded his approval at them. "Continue to use hand sanitizer. Let the office know immediately if the dispenser in your classroom has run out. No one is to use keyboards or computer components with bare hands. Boxes of latex gloves will be placed at all computer stations and in every classroom. Have students email as many assignments as possible. Germs can live on a damp piece of paper longer than you'd like to think."

The room churned at the thought of it.

"We will be suspending the attendance policy for this year's exam exemptions. We don't want to encourage kids to show up to school sick." Principal Elders narrowed his eyes. "Teachers, either. I can't stress this enough. If you're sick, stay home. If you have a fever, stay home. If you're tired, stay home. Seven days. We're hoping they come out with a flu shot for this strand soon, but it kind of snuck up on us, didn't it?"

"How come they can't predict these viruses a little better?" whispered Mr. Wellesley, the history teacher. He chewed the end of his reading glasses.

"I know. I went and got my flu shot for nothing," said Mrs. Bartish, the English Composition teacher.

"I heard Ronny Paulson has a serious case," said Ms. Simmons, the librarian. "That's why he's been absent all month."

"Thank goodness for that," Mrs. Bartish said. "My class has been so much quieter without him."

Mr. Adams bit his lip.

"Always crinkling his Scantrons," Mr. Wellesley agreed.

"And questioning everything," Ms. Alton huffed. "I hope he stays sick all year."

Mr. Adams stood suddenly. The noise around him faded into sighs. "I have a question about the standards."

Principal Elders nodded.

"The new standards don't emphasize—or test—anything having

to do with science labs."

"Is there a question?" asked Principal Elders.

"Lab work is what innovates the field of science!" Mr. Adam huffed. "If we aren't stressing discovery in the lab, then what are we—"

A chorus of groans rose in anticipation of Mr. Adam's coming tirade.

"Let me stop you there," Principal Elders said. He held his palm outward, and at the sight of it, the well-trained teachers ceased their moans. "As you know, we have state mandates to meet. If we don't, we'll lose funding. Lab work is simply one step beyond what is tested at the standardized level, so until we can get all students up to speed for the test, we simply can't afford to emphasize lab work. Or any other extraneous topic, for that matter." He moved his gaze around the auditorium to emphasize that they were all bound by his words.

"And thank goodness," whispered Mr. Pollard to Mr. Weiss, the student teacher he was training. "Standardized content is so much easier to grade. Especially in Chemistry." He adjusted his pinstripe tie and smirked.

"Can you say Scantron?" laughed Mr. Weiss.

"Not to mention all the practice tests," Pollard added. "An easy lesson if you don't want to deal with the brats."

As around him the teachers' voices rose in mumbled agreement and anecdotes, Mr. Adams turned to look at Pollard, whose face was drawn back in a permanent scowl. Mr. Adams believed it had been etched there by years of fighting students, of killing their natural curiosity through mediocrity and test scores. Pollard carried his chin raised as a haughty king might, to demonstrate that he carried a status that must not be questioned, especially by the brats that must grovel to him for their grades. He sat on the throne of mediocrity. He knew it, and he loved it.

"We'll see what the kids do with the Level Four practices," Mr. Pollard chuckled. "That'll knock 'em down a few pegs, especially Lindsey Ellers, who scored a 100 percent last time. Thinks she can teach the class now, I'll bet."

Mr. Weiss rubbed his hands. "I can't wait."

"We've ordered new workbooks for each of your classes," Principal Elders added over the low mumbles. "So each department will have a greater variety of practice tests and practice multiple-choice problems to use."

The room applauded.

Mr. Adams sat down, muttering to himself. During the rest of the meeting he scribbled furious notes on the back of his daily planner.

* * *

It took Adams only a week to create an attenuated version of the flu. His subconscious had been working on it for years: a controversial mix of virus and chemicals that one of his college professors had experimented with during the '60s. Of course it wasn't ethical. Some might even call it mind control. But old Professor Dower dubbed it "The Caterpillar Effect."

"All we're doing," he'd said, "is turning a caterpillar into a butterfly."

Regardless, Mr. Adams was well aware that what he was doing could lose him his job—or worse. Even Professor Dower had never actually tried it on humans. But the time had come. Here was the proper motivation to turn Dower's theoretical research into something tangible and practical.

Although Mr. Adams wanted to unleash it right away, he knew he should test it first. He started with Mr. Pollard, rising at dawn in order to get to school in time to break into Pollard's classroom. He used an aerated spray bottle to taint the insides of every rubber glove in Mr.

Pollard's box. Then he sprayed the virus all over the "reset" and "score" buttons on the Scantron machine in the teacher workroom. As Mr. Pollard always did his grading before classes began, it was likely that he would be the first to touch the machine and thus become the flu's first lab rat.

"Morning, Howard," Mr. Pollard said, entering the workroom. He carried a pair of latex gloves.

"Morning, Thomas." Mr. Adams was pretending to be making copies. He bit his lip to hide his excitement.

"My students scored 88 percent on the Level Two practice," Pollard said, snapping on the gloves. "Now their Level Three scores are hovering right around 80. Got to get them a bit higher."

Adams watched with delight as Pollard touched the Scantron machine and then scratched just above his eye. Then Pollard adjusted his tie. "Aiming for 90 percent."

Mr. Adams hid a smirk. "Good luck with those scores," he said, hurrying out of the workroom.

* * *

Mr. Pollard, required to take the full seven-day leave, was relieved that at least his student teacher would be there to keep his lesson plans on track. On the morning of the eighth day, Mr. Adams and Mr. Weiss were seated at tables in the workroom, grading Earth Science essays and Scantrons, when Pollard hurried in. His eyes were bright, and there was even—could Mr. Adams be imagining things?—a bounce in his step. Instead of his normal shirt and tie, Mr. Pollard wore a bright plaid shirt, a pair of khakis, and an oversized cowboy-style belt buckle embossed with the image of a series of carbon atoms playing with a lasso.

After a quick double-take, Mr. Weiss dismissed Pollard's appearance, no doubt thinking he was still recovering from his illness.

"You'll be proud of me," he beamed. "While you were gone, I followed your lesson plans exactly. We got through three practice tests. The class average rose from a 78.2 to a 79.1 percent—we're making real progress!"

Mr. Pollard looked pained. Mr. Weiss didn't notice. "Should we move on to the Level Five practice tests this week?"

Now disgust painted Pollard's face. Mr. Adams didn't need to see more. He knew the virus had worked. Still, he watched the rest of the miracle.

"Lindsey Ellers is getting pretty cocky again," Mr. Weiss prattled on, "thinking she's going to score a 100 on the next test."

Mr. Pollard held his forehead. His breathing quickened, and he glanced toward the window. He shifted from one foot to the other.

"See? Here are the score reports I printed." Mr. Weiss handed him a clipboard containing a graph and several columns of data.

Mr. Pollard took the clipboard and giggled.

"Are you all right?" Weiss asked.

Pollard giggled again and took a bright green highlighter from his pocket. He connected several points on the graph and drew three spheres.

"What anomaly did you fi—" Weiss grabbed the clipboard. There on the graph, Mr. Pollard had drawn a smiley face hovering on top of a bowtie. He connected lines at the top of the graph to form a top hat.

"That data's got a date," Pollard chuckled. "Get it? He's all dressed up." He handed the clipboard back to Mr. Weiss and ruffled the young man's hair, chuckling once more.

Mr. Adams hid a smile. He could practically see the chemicals rushing through Pollard's system.

Mr. Wellesley plodded into the room and plopped a history workbook onto the copy machine. "Welcome back, Thomas," he said, biting the end of his reading glasses. "I hear your students are on Level Four already. You've got quite the student teacher working for you!"

Mr. Weiss beamed.

Pollard frowned. "I've been thinking," he said. "All these standardized practices are boring the hell out of me. I have other plans for this week. We're going to do—some lab work."

Mr. Weiss's smile deflated.

"What?" Wellesley dropped his glasses.

"A-a-and Level Five next week, then?" Mr. Weiss stammered.

Pollard shook his head. "Not next week. We're going to have to revise the lesson plans you've turned in to the university for your student teaching credit hours. In fact, we'll need to scrap them altogether. Next week, I plan to have the kids do a bit of original research."

Mr. Wellesley twitched. "Thomas! Not with standardized testing just months away! You can't afford the time! It's a waste."

Mr. Adams tried not to hurry out of the teacher room. As much as he wanted to hear the rest of the conversation, he couldn't wait to return to his own classroom. There, in his dorm-sized refrigerator, he kept the vials. He turned them over in his hands, feeling their cool power as he read the labels: influentia bruchum. Caterpillar flu.

It wouldn't matter if the students caught it, too. Most of them had become too complacent, anyway, blindly shuffling through the curriculum for grades. Their minds could use some opening as well. He stood on his lab table and reached up to the ceiling, where an ancient intake vent rattled with the school's aging air conditioning. He pried apart a gap in the vent, opened two vials, and placed them inside. There was another vent in the cafeteria, which he could easily access during lunch duty later that day.

* * *

Mr. Adams caught the flu just before the school-wide quarantine was imposed, but as he'd been exposed to the virus already, he experienced only a day of chills, and no other side effects. When school re-opened, two weeks later, he returned to find the students more eager than usual. He wondered if it was a side effect of cabin fever or an effect of the virus.

He stopped in at the main office, where he found Mr. Elders berating the secretary. "Cookie, I told you to order one class set of these workbooks."

Cookie shook her head and pointed to an order form. "Here's the form you gave me to fax. You ordered one class set for every teacher in the school."

"Really?" Mr. Elders scratched his head and adjusted the collar on his coaching polo, a shirt he normally wore only to pep rallies. He held a stack of file folders and stared at them a moment before continuing. "Because I can't for the life of me fathom why I would do such a thing. I found a special book request from the librarian for a new fantasy series the kids have been requesting, and now it seems I've spent a good chunk of our budget on the workbooks instead."

"I'll see if they can be returned," Cookie said. "By the way, you look energized. Did you have the flu very badly?"

"Lasted almost the whole two weeks." Elders scratched his head. He was standing still, but Mr. Adams could swear the man was bouncing in his shoes. He smiled at his secretary, his whole face glowing. "And boy, did I have some weird dreams. Visions, maybe. Don't know if I was really awake or asleep. At one point, I imagined I was a student, and I was sitting in a classroom, and—" He bounced literally now, and he tapped his hand rapidly on Cookie's desk. Mr. Adams thought of a chicken trying to hatch. "I'll tell you, I never felt so

144

trapped. And I come back here to find boxes and boxes of workbooks, and—it's stifling. I keep thinking of shackles." He glared again at the stack of folders. "Can you file these reports for me, Cookie?"

"File them? Aren't those the reports you were going to analyze? Before we all got sick, you were going to call individual meetings for teachers whose practice scores hadn't increased by at least—"

Elders held his head. "Please, no more about numbers and scores. Ever since I've gotten back, I just—I can't really explain." He bit his lip. "You know what? I'll file them." He tossed the entire stack into Cookie's recycling bin, and stifled a smile.

Cookie smiled. "Just glad to have you back."

Principal Elders nodded. "Let's find the money for those fantasy books, okay?"

Mr. Adams chuckled and headed toward the bookroom. A pallet of workbooks was stacked against one wall, the plastic encasing them not even broken yet. He'd received the email notice—all the teachers had—to come pick up his class set from the pile. It seemed he wasn't the only one who had yet to do so.

Students lined the hallways, and as he walked by, Mr. Adams caught snippets of their conversations.

" . . . is cancelling the research paper and letting us write a collection of short stories instead. And Lindsey Ellers is even going to try writing a novel! This is gonnabe hard as hell."

" . . . said for our final exam, he's entering us in a team physics competition. We'll have to build a rocket that can weigh no more than ten pounds, but that has to travel all the way to . . . "

" . . . if we can write a first-person account from one of the major players of World War I, including footnoted facts, she won't make us take the next unit test . . . "

" . . . told her it would be easier just to take the damned multiple choice test. The project requires too much effort. Don't know what kind of crack these teachers are on, but . . . "

". . . working with the art students to make a movie teaching lower-level math students how factoring works. We're going to use little critters called Math-Mites that one of the artists drew, and we're going to . . . "

". . . I'd saved all my sister's Scantrons from last year, but now he says we're having an essay test instead. I hate this."

"I've been copying Mel, and getting by that way, but now we're switching to essay tests! I'm gonna fail."

"You could always actually read the chapters."

Mr. Adams smiled at the mixture of excitement and fear in the students' voices. He was even glad for the ones who were angry. Anger was far better than apathy—any day. It meant they cared. The bell rang, but Mr. Adams had his planning period during the first block, so he walked the halls to peek in on the various classrooms, stopping at the door of Mr. Pollard's class.

The room was quiet, students' eyes widening as Mr. Pollard explained the original research project they'd be assigned for the following quarter. Instead of standing behind the podium as straight as his tie, he soared from row to row of student desks in his colorful new outfit, almost like a butterfly. A few of his students even seemed to be scribbling ideas on the inside cover of their daily planners.

Mr. Adams turned and headed back down the hall, passing the book storage room, where the brand-new copies of Level Six practice workbooks were already gathering dust.

Unintended Lesson

George G. Moore

In the last row of the auditorium-like lecture hall, Ryan took a seat beside his roommate, Vinny. From his backpack, he pulled out his Econ textbook, notebook, and a pen. He looked around to the other students and shook his head. A few were asleep, their heads tilted at awkward angles. Others fiddled with their cell phones while the tabletop before them remained spotless. They were going to have problems—by all accounts, Econ was a difficult subject.

Another student entered, and Ryan could tell immediately that he was a loser. His jeans were ripped, and he wore sandals. Even his t-shirt was wrinkled to the point that it looked as if it had been worn before.

And his hair was . . . thinning? He had to be in his thirties. What kind of student was this? A moment later, Ryan had his answer. Instead of taking a seat, he stood behind the lectern.

"Welcome to Economics 101, Introduction to Macroeconomics. I'm Professor Rogers. This course is required to earn any degree in this university. The Thursday classes will start with a ten question quiz worth 100 points covering the previous Monday and Thursday's lectures and assigned readings. You'll have fifteen minutes to complete it, and you can earn partial credit for all questions. Afterward, I'll lecture. A mid-term and final will replace the Thursday quizzes for those weeks, and you'll have the entire class time to complete them."

Vinny leaned over to Ryan and whispered, "Damn, this guy thinks Econ is the center of the universe."

"Shh."

Professor Rogers continued. "As part of this course, we'll also survey several economic systems such as communism, socialism, and capitalism. While each is flawed, I intend to demonstrate how socialism is the best way to handle economic matters. By the end of this course, you see that cooperation will always produce more benefits than competition, which taken to its logical conclusion means destroying every competitor. In that spirit, I'm thrilled to offer you a new option regarding grading. We can do standard grading, no curve, or I can give each of you the average of everyone's score. This way, you can work together in cooperation to share the fruits of your collective efforts. Please raise your hand if you wish to receive the average of everyone's grade."

Hands went up, lots of hands. Those who a few minutes earlier had been distracted or asleep, thrust their hands upward.

"Quick, check out who hasn't raised their hands. See if you know them." Ryan looked around. Down three rows and to his left, Jeff and Joni sat with their hands down, frowning at one another.

With a broad smile on his face, Professor Rogers looked around. "Congratulations! You'll each receive the average of everyone's score. I know you'll achieve so much by working together, for the common good. Now, before I forget, read chapters one through five for Thursday's quiz."

Vinny leaned over and said, "I caught sight of Steve and Peter. Why does it matter?"

"I'm afraid we have a problem."

* * *

Ryan strode through the double doors of the library's main entrance. As he expected, it was nearly deserted. These days, students didn't bother researching at the library but preferred to use the computers in their dorm rooms. For him and a few others, it was a quiet refuge to think and study.

At a table in the corner, Joni sat. As usual, Jeff was by her side. Today, Joni's friend, Lori, had joined them. He didn't know Lori well, but she'd struck him as level-headed and bright. If she was hanging out in the library, odds were that she'd be interested in what he had to say.

He drew near and interrupted their animated conversation. "Hey, guys. You have a minute?"

In unison, they looked up. Jeff had a sour look on his face. Lori didn't look much happier. Joni frowned, and her cheeks were red, too.

"Sure," Jeff said. "Maybe you can help. We're arguing about Econ."

Ryan sat next to Lori, facing Joni and Jeff. "That's what's on my mind, too."

"This class is going to go south," Joni said. "Human nature will take over."

Jeff stared at Joni. "C'mon, all of our classmates met the admissions' requirements. They're smart. They won't let us down."

"Bullshit," Joni said, barely stifling her voice from echoing through library as her blond bangs bounced against her forehead. "There's a reason they voted for it. They think they'll do better with the class's grade than their own. And because the majority voted for it, what do you think their grade'll be?"

"Poor." Ryan swallowed hard. "You're right, Joni. These folks think they're getting something for nothing. They failed to realize that Rogers removed the incentive to achieve, so very few will do the work, thinking that others will."

"Are you going to do less work?" Jeff asked. "I'm not."

"Neither am I," Ryan said. "But, I have my eye on landing a good job, not simply passing while waiting for the next party."

No one spoke for a moment. With Joni's observations, the problem had come into sharper focus, and it was worse than he'd thought. The problem wasn't a mediocre grade—it was failing the class, which wouldn't put him on the path to a good job.

Lori pushed several strands of long, brown hair behind her right ear. "There's no doubt that some will slack off. What about the innocent students caught in the middle, the ones working hard just to pass?"

Joni inhaled deeply. "They're gonna get hurt, probably give up when they see the writing on the wall. There's nothing we can do for them. Those who voted for the proposal will get what they deserve. The rest will be victims of an uninformed majority. Make no mistake, everyone will fail."

Jeff shook his head.

Ryan nodded. "It'll feed on itself. If we do nothing, we're toast. Taking action based on nothing but our low opinions of our classmates isn't wise, though."

Jeff said, "Let's see what happens on the first couple of quizzes."

Lori smiled as she looked at Jeff. "Let's hold study groups. The library has meeting rooms. We'll take turns running them."

"Good idea. I'll be glad to lead one." Jeff returned her smile.

"Okay, I'll create and post notices," Lori said, looking to Joni, almost daring her to object.

"It won't make a difference." A single look wasn't about to dissuade her.

"You're probably right, Joni, but Lori has a good idea. It may avoid some nasty consequences if it works. We need to try it." Ryan leaned forward. "But, if it doesn't work, here's what I think we should do."

For the next minute, Ryan laid out his plan. Lori sighed, and Jeff's face was expressionless. Joni pursed her lips and nodded.

* * *

Two weeks later, in the library, at the same isolated corner table, Ryan rubbed his eyes, wondering why he was working so hard.

"You, okay?" Joni asked.

"Yeah, I suppose."

"You look awful. What's wrong?"

"I'm rereading about the Laffer curve, and a thought struck me. Why does it matter? We got a 73 on the second quiz—that's the bottom of average. It makes me thankful for the 84 on the first quiz."

After laying her highlighter down, Joni glared at him. "Thankful for an 84? We each earned a 96 on that quiz. This last one, I earned a 95. I'm not thankful. I'm pissed."

"I'm at 'discouraged.' I'm working my way up to 'pissed.'" Ryan forced a grin. "The trend's heading in the wrong direction. I don't have a good feeling about tomorrow's quiz."

With a sigh, Jeff settled in beside Joni, depositing his backpack on the table.

"How'd the study session go yesterday?" Ryan asked.

"Great," Jeff said in a monotone. "Everyone there will do wonderfully on tomorrow's quiz."

Ryan tried to make sense of Jeff's statement in conjunction with his tone.

Jeff shook his head. "I was the only one there."

"I had two attend my session," Joni said. "To their credit, they were eager to learn. One expressed regret afterward that she voted for the grading system."

"No one showed for mine." Ryan said.

Vinny slid into the chair to Ryan's right. "Hey, guys. I know what's going on behind the scenes. After some digging on the Internet, I discovered that Rogers won a pilot program grant from the Department of Education to implement alternate grading methods as means to increase productivity."

Joni pursed her lips and shook her head. "Unbelievable. Who would've guessed—Rogers likes money just like the rest of us."

For Ryan, the slim hope of avoiding the consequences of Professor Rogers' grading policy had just died. Not only were Rogers' personal beliefs involved, money was at stake. He'd never alter his grading policy.

A few seconds passed before Jeff spoke. "That explains my conversation with the dean this morning. He refuses to give us the grades we earn. He says that he fully supports Professor Roger's grading policy."

"Of course he does," Joni said with a disgusted look on her face. "He's slurping away at the government trough right beside Rogers. I'll bet you there's grant money for the school and for each of them to administer the program, too."

"It's worse than that. The grant specified that we had to volunteer for the grading system—Rogers couldn't impose it. The rationale is that we'll make it work because we wanted it." Vinny paused and looked at each of them. "Don't you get it? We're an experiment, sponsored and approved by the government. Some faceless bureaucrat wants an answer to his pet question. He doesn't care what it does to us or our career prospects. We're nothing more than Guinea pigs."

"I've had it with this class," Joni said, red-faced, her anger barely contained.

"I second that," Ryan said quietly. "We might as well take

tomorrow's quiz and gauge our classmates' reaction."

"You know they're gonna be shocked shitless. We're long past common sense pointing to the correct answers." Joni stared at Jeff for a few moments. Afterward, she looked at Vinny. "Pass this information along to Peter and Steve, and let's have a meeting to decide once and for all our course of action. Procrastinating won't make what needs to be done any easier."

Jeff said flatly, "I agree."

Joni looked at him with her mouth agape. Ryan couldn't believe his ears, either.

"You guys were right—I was wrong. Our classmates are screwing us."

Vinny smiled. "About time you got on board."

"Jeff, it's okay." Ryan did his best to smile. "This is one time I wanted to be wrong."

"I told you so," Joni said, her eyes wide. "You see the best in everyone and everything. You gotta get your head outta the clouds and deal with what's before us."

Between Jeff disagreeing with her and her irritation with Econ, Joni wasn't letting Jeff off the hook. Ryan sympathized with him and hoped that he hung in a little time longer—Joni would get over it.

"Joni, once the quiz is over, we'll know exactly where we stand. We can make an informed decision." Ryan saw the path before them. No matter how hard he tried to avoid it, they were walking it. And at its end, many people would be displeased.

* * *

A single, soft rap followed by two quicker raps sounded on Ryan's dorm room door. Ryan looked up, rose from the uncomfortable wooden stool, and cracked the door. "Come in, Jeff."

As Ryan shut the door, Jeff sat beside Joni on Ryan's bed. Lori sat at a desk, staring at its top. On the opposite side of the room, Vinny sat on his bed. Steve sat at the other desk, and Peter leaned against the wall near the door. Crammed into the room, they assembled to decide their next move.

Ryan inhaled deeply. None of them were pleased with the situation, and it showed in their grim expressions. "Okay, we're all here. In short, the situation is this: The grade trend is heading into the toilet. Rogers won't change his grading policy, and the dean stands behind him because they're participating in a government program, which is providing big bucks."

"Yes, yes, we all know that," Joni said impatiently. "We took the third quiz last Thursday, and we'll get our grades—our failing grades— tomorrow. Now, what are we gonna do? I'm tired of waiting for all of you to decide. I'm ready to go it alone."

"And that's why we're here. It's best for all of us to agree and move in concert. Perhaps, by doing so, we'll make a statement, so no one else has to go through this again."

Joni frowned but didn't argue, and Ryan was thankful. Since hearing about the government grant, mentally, he'd joined her, and if all went as expected tonight, everyone else would, too. The key was for their friends to reach the conclusion for themselves, not force it on them.

Vinny glanced at Joni and said, "Before we decide anything, let's get all our questions out in the open, so we're making decisions based on facts, not emotions."

Lori raised her head and looked at Vinny. "I know Jeff and Ryan didn't have any takers for their study sessions. Joni had two. How about you, Vinny?"

"None. From what I hear, there was a wild party in Stevens Hall. I'll bet anything the majority of our class was there."

Peter laughed. "No bet. I popped in and recognized at least two dozen of our classmates. Thank God Econ's an afternoon class. They wouldn't have made a morning class, not sober anyway."

Vinny added, "Maybe they'd score better drunk."

Ryan shot him a dirty look. He was in no mood for lame jokes. "Based on that and my classroom observations, I believe the odds that we passed the last quiz are slim."

"Just passing is shit for the birds," Joni said, her face red with anger. "I pulled a 'C' on the second quiz when I'm doing 'A' work. And I'll tell you something else: I don't care about the party in Stevens—there's a party in Stevens every night. They need discipline to study, and that's beyond our control."

As Ryan ran his hand through his hair, he sighed. "I agree."

"I've spoken with several of our classmates, trying to get them to attend a study session," Lori said. "Some say the work's too hard. Others are discouraged because no matter how much effort they put in, their grades are slipping. A few told me—to my face, mind you—that us high I.Q. types will save the day because we're in the same boat as them. They weren't concerned at all."

Jeff rubbed his temples. "Bad at Econ and horrible at basic math all wrapped in a neat little bow. Beautiful . . . "

Still leaning against the wall, Peter asked, "Ryan, your dad's in the Diplomatic Corp and an alumnus. Can he use his connections to help us?"

Ryan shook his head. "We don't see eye to eye. If we did, I'd be walking off San Diego beaches to attend classes, not sitting in the mountains of western Pennsylvania. For the record, though, I tried. I spoke with him after the first class, before I approached any of you. He insisted that I grow up and solve my own problems."

His father had acted as if he'd been whining about a run-of-the-mill annoyance, not facing an extraordinarily unfair situation. Nothing he'd said changed his father's mind.

After subtly shaking her head, Joni said, "The simple fact is that we're on our own. We aren't getting any help from our parents or the administration. Any more questions?"

No one spoke. Peter and Lori shook their heads.

Ryan straightened his shoulders and inhaled. "Unless we're willing to fail, I see only one option. Raise your hand if you want to go through with our plan."

In silence, everyone raised a hand.

It was decided.

* * *

Ryan located his graded quiz on the lectern. He glanced at it and exhaled before climbing the steep aisle and taking his seat in the back of the lecture hall.

Professor Rogers entered and strode to the lectern. He switched on the mike and adjusted it. "I'm very disappointed. As a class, you earned a 54, which is failing. There's no reason for such a low score. Your combined resources should easily be netting you 'A's. All of you need to work together for the collective good. This irrational urge that some of you have to go it alone, withhold your talents from the whole, harms the entire class. The dean and I have had a handful of students approach us to receive their individual grades, not the class's grade. Make no mistake, they're selfish. They're only looking out for themselves. They don't care about anyone else. They're the reason why the class grade is so low. Just so it's perfectly clear, I won't change the grading policy, nor will I make exceptions to it. You will work together, and you will succeed."

And it was clear. Rogers had just laid the groundwork to blame the small group who was producing for the whole group's failure. Ryan and his friends were teed up for the role of scapegoat. It was an old trick that, sadly, worked. Rogers counted on the class finding it easier to blame someone else than to reason.

To his core, Ryan felt his resolve harden. What he and his friends planned was absolutely right; no doubt remained.

"Now, let's look at question three," Rogers continued. "Most of you had difficulty with it."

Ryan tuned out Rogers droning on about the multiple shortcomings of supply-side economic theory—according to him, anyway. While he might've received a 54 on the quiz, he'd earned a 92, which was marked in red at the top of the page.

From two rows down and a handful of seats to his left, Joni turned and stared at him with a grim expression on her face. Ryan grimaced and nodded once. She returned the nod before turning back and whispering in Jeff's ear.

After seeing Rogers in action, Ryan was pleased that Joni had heeded his advice to move with the group. A couple of hours from now, their classmates would despise them, possibly most of the student body. They'd only have each other for support.

As soon as class ended, Ryan shouldered his backpack and exited through the rear door. He took the stairs down. What he and his friends were about to do left a bitter taste in his mouth, but they'd exhausted every alternative. He just wanted to get it over with.

Before he knew it, he was on the ground floor, the flight of stairs a blur. He departed the building and hastened along the concrete path dividing the manicured campus lawns. In the distance, past the dormitory halls and educational buildings, he saw the Administration building where he'd meet the others.

"Ryan, Hold up!"

It sounded like Peter. Perhaps he'd found an option that they hadn't considered. Ryan stopped and turned.

Instead, it was Tad Williams, an up-and-coming point guard, running toward him. "Hey, Ryan, I'm glad I caught you."

"Whatcha need?"

"You and your brain friends need to get your act together. I'm going to lose my eligibility if you don't raise our score."

Ryan jammed his hands in his sweatshirt pockets. "There's nothing that we can do about that."

Tad stepped closer, his nose within inches of Ryan's face. "I'm not stupid. I know better than that."

Tad might not be stupid, but he failed to work all the way through the math. At least, Tad didn't outright threaten him. There might be hope for him yet. Ryan squared his shoulders. "The first thing you need to understand is that intimidation doesn't work with me. Neither do threats. Now, step back so we can have a civilized discussion."

Tad's eyes grew wide, but he took one step back.

"Good. Whether the brains work harder or not, your eligibility's still screwed. It has been since day one."

"I don't have time for brain teasers. I need a passing grade."

"Have your coach fix it for you." Ryan was sure that Tad had already tried it. He was curious why it didn't work.

Tad glanced over Ryan's shoulder. "I'm not a starter. As it stands, if I fail off the team, five people just as good are waiting to replace me."

Ryan had never cared much for jocks, but ultimately they were performance-based, one of the few holdouts in an otherwise entitled society, and he appreciated that quality. "Your problem's with Rogers, not the brains. I'll be happy to explain why everyone is destined to fail and has been since day one. And, I'll tell you the only way to salvage your eligibility."

Tad's eyebrows drew closer as he asked, "Whatcha mean?"

"What'd you get on the quiz?"

"A 68."

"That's below average."

"Yeah, but good enough to maintain my eligibility."

Ryan frowned. "Did you study at all?"

"A couple of hours after basketball practice Wednesday night."

"While we studied, a sizable portion of the class partied at Stevens Hall. Sounds like more fun than studying, huh?"

"Sure. So what?"

"It's just something to keep in mind. We worked hard, they partied hard, but we all received the same grade. That doesn't sound fair to me."

Tad tilted his head slightly. "How is this saving my eligibility?"

Ryan wondered what Tad would do after school. The odds stated that he probably wouldn't make it as a pro. Didn't he realize that his free education in exchange for playing ball was the best backup plan? "Skip it. I scored a 92. To keep the math simple, let's assume that I had the high score, and there was only one other, not one hundred, taking the quiz. That means the low score is . . . ." Ryan paused a moment to do the calculation.

"Around twelve, a little more."

"Actually, it's sixteen, but that's a decent off-the-cuff answer." Ryan's eyebrows rose—Tad had some brains. Perhaps he'd grasp the truth. "Let's say I study hard and score a perfect 100. That only raises the average to 58. We still fail. You see that, right?"

"Yeah," Tad said and let out a long sigh.

"I don't have much upside, but consider the loser scoring a sixteen. If he doubles his score, he still earns a failing grade, but the average grade rises to 62, a lousy grade, but a passing one."

"Hey, great point. Thanks. I'll catch you later." Tad turned back toward the classroom.

"Tad, I can't let you go. You can't get the partiers and the lazy to put in more effort. Why would they? They're getting something for nothing. Even if you explicitly threaten them, you can't follow through with enough to make a difference before the administration hears about it and expels you."

"C'mon, you were supposed to tell me how to maintain my eligibility." His jaw tensed. Clearly, between the conversation and the class, the stress was weighing on him.

"Let's walk." Ryan guided him toward the Administration building. He noticed Jeff, Joni, and Lori ahead on the path, wondered for a moment when they'd passed him, and decided it didn't matter. "The scores are gonna get worse. The top seven students are dropping the class today."

"Are you insane? Our scores'll nosedive!"

Ryan smiled and glanced over to Tad. "They don't have to. The rest of your classmates could do the work. But, realistically speaking, you're right."

"You selfish bastards. Just because you aren't getting your precious 'A's, you quit."

"Selfish? Aren't our classmates the selfish ones, expecting us to work while they do nothing to contribute, yet reap the rewards of our efforts? Remember, at least one slub earned a sixteen—there were probably several. We posted notices for study groups to prep for the quizzes. Two people showed. Like you, we can't force them to do their work."

"Explain it to them, like you just did to me. They'll do the work."

"Again, they're getting something for nothing. There's no individual incentive, and most importantly, there's no individual accountability." Ryan paused for a moment and shook his head. "No, they're gonna get what they deserve: failure. They placed their fate in others' hands, people who can't care for them as much as they care about themselves."

"Damn, you're serious."

"I'm offended by Rogers and the grading system. I'm deeply disappointed that so many were seduced by it. You should be, too."

Tad opened his mouth, but hesitated for a moment. "Why?"

"Does anyone shoot your free throws for you? Does anyone guard your man for you? Does anyone practice for you?"

Tad stopped and turned to Ryan, who also stopped. "No. I busted my ass to get here. I spent hours practicing and training. I have to do even more to get to the next level."

"The brains, as you call us, worked hard to get where we are. For us to reach the next level, we have to do even more. That means that we put in the effort to earn excellent grades. We don't want people who don't know us and couldn't care less about us to hold us back."

Ryan took a step toward Tad. He was easily within arm's reach. "The only way out of this mess is to drop the class, eat a chunk of the tuition, and take Econ 101 with a different prof. Our classmates failed to recognize the grading scheme for what it was—yet another example of a policy that has failed every single time it has ever been tried. Our classmates are about to learn a lesson that Rogers never meant to teach.

"Tad, you don't have to learn this lesson the hard way. See the situation for what it truly is. Walk with me to the registrar's office. Join with the brains, drop the class, and take control of your future."

For a long moment, Tad stood, staring at Ryan. By the look on his face, he was working through the situation. He nodded and looked to the Administration building. "It's the only way, isn't it?"

BROKEN CONTROL

Natasha Bennett

Wait until after two a.m., then sneak in. That's when their patrols will be weakest. Remember, I want the brunette.

Moving quietly as a shadow, Jeff ran up the dark stairs of the broken hotel and stopped behind a pillar as he spotted a man near the window, smoking a cigarette. His heart pounded as he carefully maneuvered around him and made his way through an open doorway. In the next room, he could see five people asleep in various bedding— some of them on a mattress, others in sleeping bags. The roof had caved in at some point, but the dark sky was overcast, and he wouldn't be easily seen. He didn't see anyone protecting them. Perfect.

It wasn't hard to find the woman Gaius was looking for. She was sleeping on a single cover only, her head tilted at an uncomfortable angle. Her brown hair was disheveled over her face, but what immediately drew his eye was her body. The woman wore a dark-blue silken shirt which only barely seemed to contain the size of her bust. Part of her shirt was ripped, revealing a tanned shoulder. Jeff could see why Gaius wanted her. The thought made him angry, but only briefly. After the nuclear bombs fell, breaking the world apart, the flesh market became a lucrative trade.

Jeff took out a silver collar which glinted in the moonlight. The smooth metal hummed under his fingertips; it wasn't a typical collar. Gaius told him it was a prototype of some sort. Once a person wore this, they never wanted to wear anything else ever again. It looked like a good fit for her neck. He stepped forward, almost tripping on a loose piece of cement. Slowly, he lowered himself down to her body, collar at the ready.

Suddenly, he felt something sharp tickling his ribs. The tip of a gun. "Nice try, honey," she said, her eyes opening. Even though he wanted to piss his pants with fear, he was drawn to the distinct features on her face—her blue eyes looked too small, with dark shadows underneath. She gave him a crooked smile. "Who are you?"

"I—I . . . " Jeff stammered.

"Oh shit, we've got another slaver?" a man in his late seventies asked, struggling out of his bag. Despite his age, his muscles were bulging and covered with scars, and he studied Jeff with clear eyes. This was an old geezer who wouldn't lose his marbles anytime soon. Beside him a teenage girl was wiping sleep from her eyes.

Jeff's blood boiled with indignation. "What are you talking about? I'm not a slaver!"

"Oh really?" the woman asked mockingly. She gestured with her gun. "You just wanted to sneak into our little fortress in the middle of the night for . . . what, a coffee and a chat?" She shook the inert collar. "With this?"

"No, I . . . " Jeff felt his cheeks burning with shame. They were right. In a sense, he was a slaver now. He had failed her. There was no turning back.

"Who sent you?" the woman asked, waving her gun. "Obviously you're not the brains of this operation, and we've had three slavers hit us in the last week alone."

Jeff looked up, alarmed. There was no way in hell he would tell her. "No one."

"Did I mention that we threw the previous slavers through the window?" She gestured at a broken pane of glass. "They didn't survive."

Jasmine! Jeff's heart lurched in his chest. He was never going to see her again. "If you're going to kill me, just do it already," he snapped. "I have nothing to say to you."

For a moment, the woman studied him, uncertain. "You're not acting like a normal slaver," she muttered. "Most of them would be trying to buy their lives with money by now."

"Sucks to be me, I guess," Jeff retorted, angrily meeting her gaze. "I don't have any."

"Who are you working for?"

"No one. I fully intended to sell you on the black market by myself," Jeff stated.

The woman studied him. "You're lying."

"What do you want to do with him?" the old man asked, touching the woman's shoulder.

"What's your name?" the woman asked.

"Jeff."

"Jeff. Okay, fine. My name's Amanda. Not that I'm entirely sure you care to know it, given how you were just fine to sell me like a piece of meat a few minutes ago. You're a puzzle to me, Mr. Jeff, one that I don't have time to figure out." She smiled her crooked smile. "Fortunately, there is a very easy way to get the truth. And it'll give you a taste of your own medicine, I suppose."

"Amanda, what are you doing?" the older man asked.

"I've heard about these new collars, Gregory. They can make someone tell the truth," Amanda said. "Now shut up."

"Amanda, maybe we shouldn't do this." Amanda ignored

Gregory as she clamped the collar around Jeff's neck, which hummed under his skin.

Suddenly, Jeff was transported to another place entirely. It was as though his mind was disconnected from his body and floating somewhere else—a place where there was no pain. He didn't want to leave this place. This was better than any drug he could possibly take.

"Who do you work for?" a voice whispered, seemingly out of nowhere and everywhere at the same time.

"Gaius Arving." The words tumbled out of his lips before he even realized that he had spoken. After he said them, however, he didn't really care.

"Shit," Gregory said. "Whatever you did to piss him off this time, Amanda, you've succeeded."

"I broke up a few of his supply lines here and there," Amanda said, amused.

Jeff's eyes remained closed. In his mind, he was floating through a cloud. Unless they asked him a question or gave him a direction, he was content to simply sit and wait. For the rest of his life, if necessary.

"You said you were not a slaver. What did you mean by that?" Amanda asked.

Once, that question might have meant something to him. Not anymore. "Three months ago, Gaius Arving kidnapped my daughter. She is only eight years old. I . . . I didn't have enough money to buy her back. He said that if I could find a suitable replacement, the money I had would be sufficient. He wanted you."

"So you've never been a slaver before?" Gregory asked

Jeff frowned. For some reason the question bothered him, although he couldn't remember why. "No. I'm a car mechanic."

"That's great. Just brilliant," a young, teenage female voice

166

spoke, one which Jeff didn't recognize. "No wonder we couldn't recognize any of the men Gaius sent after us lately. No wonder he never seems to run out."

Suddenly, Jeff felt a soft hand grab the collar around his neck and he was yanked forwards as it fell off. He blinked as reality came crashing down on him. A second later, his cheek exploded in pain as Amanda slapped him. A drop of blood fell from his mouth and landed on the dusty ground below. "I . . . " he stammered. "I'm sorry. I didn't want to do this."

"Where is Gaius' camp?" Amanda asked.

But Jeff shook his head. No. That was too much to ask.

Amanda grinned ruefully and lifted the collar. "We can always put this back on."

"Amanda!" Gregory snapped, gripping her shoulder. "I want to talk to you. *Now.*"

Annoyed, Amanda glanced at the others. "Keep an eye on him," she ordered.

* * *

A few minutes later Amanda stormed onto the rooftop with Gregory right on her heels. The sun would be up in a couple of hours, but for now Amanda could barely see anything past the back of her hand. It didn't matter—she had seen the same view for the past eight months. Beyond the rooftop they would see an endless stretch of desert punctuated by the occasional broken car, or road. If she searched hard enough, she might find the occasional stray carcass. Such was the result of nuclear warfare.

"What?"

"Laying it on him a bit thick, aren't we?" Gregory asked. "He's not Gaius, my dear."

Amanda snorted. "He's scum, but he was sneaky. One of these

days the slavers will get past me, you know. What if he had gone after Tanya instead? She's too young to know how to defend herself."

"Not that young," Gregory said, sticking his hands in his pockets. "None of us are, anymore."

"I need answers," Amanda persisted. "Or else Gaius is going to send someone else again, and again. Frankly I'm getting tired of throwing people out of windows."

Gregory rubbed his grizzled white jaw. "He wants you bad, doesn't he?"

Amanda studied him coldly. "Is that a problem?" she asked. They had been close friends for the past nine years and always fought together side by side. The others they had picked up along the way. But they lived in a world where resources were few and far between. If Gregory chose to leave because of her private little war, then she wouldn't blame him.

But Gregory smiled, surprising her. "I am merely suggesting," he said, "that there are easier ways to gain answers from our new friend here. He doesn't seem like a bad guy. Perhaps we can talk to him?"

Amanda frowned. "That doesn't sound easier," she grumbled.

* * *

Jeff sat with his back to the wall, fighting a wave of tears that threatened to blur his vision. He had screwed up royally this time. Maybe if he was lucky, they would let him go, but he was no closer to saving his daughter.

"My name's Tanya. What is she like?" the teenager girl asked him. "Your daughter?"

Jeff shrugged, smiling a little. "Beautiful. A little malnourished. After the bombs fell . . . well, there wasn't much work for a guy who fixed cars for a living. I collected a few jobs here and there, but after that . . . ." He trailed off. "Unless you're a slaver or a trader with an army to back you up, most people around here just survive. They don't flourish."

Tanya nodded. "It feels like that here."

They looked up as Amanda returned. "Give us a minute, won't you?" she asked.

"Great. Smoke break," Tanya said.

"In your dreams." When she was alone with Jeff, Amanda folded her arms. "It occurs to me that you don't fully understand the situation, so let me explain it to you. I have more reason to hate Gaius than anyone else. The man is the biggest slaver in this country and pure evil, but my hatred runs deeper than that. I will gladly murder any of his friends and family, even if they did nothing wrong. If I could string up his associates and place them on a cross just to get his attention, I would. Hell, if a mosquito bit him and I had a chance to swat it, I would. Because then I would have a chance to kill a part of him."

"What did he do to you?" Jeff asked.

"None of your business," Amanda snapped. "My associate thinks that I crossed a line with you. Honestly, I don't see why, but you have two choices. You can either help me and tell me where Gaius's camp is, or I can kill you like the rest and hopefully send a message."

"And if I just want to leave?" Jeff asked.

"Sorry, not an option."

"Helping you won't help my daughter," Jeff said.

Amanda lowered her head, considering that. "If I can get to Gaius's camp, I will make it a priority to set free anyone trapped there . . . assuming they haven't been sold." Her blue eyes narrowed. "Assuming, of course, I know where the camp is to begin with."

Jeff hesitated. "Well, in that case . . . I guess I'll take the first option."

* * *

Over the next week, most of the people at the hotel treated Jeff as a friend, not a prisoner. During the day, Gregory taught him how to fire a rifle. Even though he nearly dislocated his shoulder the first time, he soon got the hang of it. At night Tanya was supposed to be watching him, but instead they sneaked away to share a few smokes.

Amanda, on the other hand, watched Jeff like a hawk. Jeff got a sense that the closer he was to the others, the more it irritated her. Finally, after one night when she screamed at Tanya for spilling the water, Jeff decided he had enough.

"What is your problem?" he demanded after everyone else had gone to bed and she was standing watch at the top of the tower.

Amanda ignored him for a minute as she cleaned her shotgun. "We're going to be raiding Gaius's camp tomorrow," she stated. "You should get some rest while you still can. After that, we both get what we want, and we can go our separate ways."

"And what if I want something more?" Jeff asked.

Surprised, Amanda glanced at him.

"I've spent the last few years stripping down cars and selling the parts just to have enough food for my daughter. You people have a great set-up here. You have supplies, a great defense . . . even if I find my daughter, we might be attacked by another slaver at any time."

"It's not such a great defense," Amanda muttered. "You got through."

"I'm not the man you think I am, Amanda," Jeff snapped, rubbing a hand through his grizzled cheek. "Give me half a chance and I can prove that."

Amanda laughed curtly. "Yes you are. You're all the same." She scowled. "I don't like you, Jeff. you're not my type."

"What is your type?" Jeff stepped closer. "Huh?"

"A man who's in control of his life." The words left her in one breath, and she looked disgusted with herself as soon as she said it.

"I am in control. Amanda . . . " He reached for her, and she looked up at him in terror.

All of a sudden he felt a *click* around his neck. *The collar*, he thought in horror. She put the collar around—it was the last thought he had before his world abruptly turned into gray, and he couldn't think at all.

Amanda's lips curved into a smile, and she giggled. "Really? Let's find out. Bark like a dog."

Jeff wanted to fight it, except he couldn't remember what he was fighting. He happily barked.

"What's going on?" Tanya asked as she opened the door.

Amanda waved a dismissive hand. "It's fine, Tanya. Jeff and I are just doing an experiment to see how far we can push the boundaries of this collar." She focused her cold blue eyes on her. "Leave us."

There was a long pause. "Um . . . okay," Tanya said, and left.

Amanda snorted as the door closed, then moved closer until her lips were close to his ear. "I don't know if you can even understand me with that collar on," she hissed. "But had you succeeded, this is the life you would have forced upon me."

She grinned and stepped back. "So do some work for me, *slave*," she said, spreading her arms. "Finish up cleaning my shotgun."

With his mind in a haze, Jeff expertly disassembled the shotgun, cleaned it, and reassembled it within two minutes.

Amanda silently watched him. "So you still remember what Gregory taught you. Interesting." She bit her lower lip. "Break the index finger on your right hand."

Jeff heard something crack as his left hand moved to his right, but he couldn't feel the slightest bit of pain.

Amanda studied his reaction, her eyes wide. Seeing nothing from him, she moved a hand to her mouth to stifle a giggle. She hesitated, then ran up to him and kissed him savagely on the lips. She then drew back, watching his reaction. She frowned as she saw none, and then her face lit up. "Love me," she ordered.

A loud explosion broke through the clouds in his mind. For a few seconds, the noise was powerful enough to break through his haze, and he could see Gregory standing behind them. He was holding a smoking gun, pointed upwards into the sky.

His face was vivid. "You . . . .*you dare!*"

Amanda stumbled forwards. "Gregory . . . it's . . . it's not—"

He back-handed her, powerful enough for her to pitch to the left, along the edge of the wall. Never stopping, Gregory grabbed Jeff under the arm. Jeff wasn't in any condition to resist—already his mind was starting to fade again, and his vision blurred. Back to the clouds. The pretty clouds . . . .

It might have been minutes, or hours later as Jeff could feel the collar pull away from him. Without thinking, he reached for it with a ragged cry. Scowling, Gregory pushed him back on . . . something. A metal table. It took a few seconds for Jeff to comprehend where he was. He was sitting in a dark room with only a few candles for illumination. He could see a few bandages on the shelf, and a closed cupboard, but that was it. As he watched, Gregory slammed the collar on the ground, grabbed a baseball bat, and smashed it to bits.

"Good riddance," the old man whispered. Seeing his bemused look, Gregory explained, "the more you wear it, the more you want to keep it on. Eventually you would have starved to death."

Jeff touched his broken finger. To his surprise, it had been set with a small cast wrapped around it. "Where am I?"

"The basement. It's my medical room. It's not much, but I can still fix broken bones and bullet wounds."

"You used to be a doctor?"

Gregory nodded. "Even at my age, Gaius would kill for someone like me. Not that I am particularly interested in his employment." He gave the collar one last hit. "I have to apologize for Amanda's behavior. I wanted to think that we were above acting like most of the barbarians we run into, but I can see that Amanda has proven me wrong . . . " His fists clenched. " . . . .despite her circumstances. Are you okay?"

Jeff nodded. "Yes, I think so. What circumstances? What are you talking about?"

"I suppose it's more than fair to tell you given her behavior," Gregory said with a heavy sigh. "Years ago, while we were scavenging supplies, Gaius raped her. He came out of nowhere, and by the time we doubled back, the damage had already been done. He made her feel unworthy to be a human being."

"Jesus," Jeff whispered. "So I guess treating her like an object wouldn't exactly leave a favorable reaction."

"That's a correct assumption, yes," Gregory said, lifting a needle and flicking the bubbles out. He stabbed it into Jeff's arm. "Painkiller. Look kid, Amanda crossed the line. If you wanted to leave the hotel tonight, no one will stop you."

But Jeff shook his head. "I want to talk to her." He glanced at the destroyed collar. "You don't have more of those things laying around, do you?"

"No."

"Good." Jeff shivered, then stood. "Thanks. For everything."

Gregory sighed. "Kid, we have to look out for each other. It's the only chance we have."

* * *

Jeff found Amanda exactly where he had left her—on the rooftop of the hotel. She was sitting on a bench, her gaze uncertain. As he slammed open the door, she stood, shaken. "Jeff," she began. "What

I did—"

"Crossed a few lines. I know," Jeff said. "So did I, when I came here. Amanda, I'm not going to hurt you like he did, I swear. And I know a way into Gaius's compound, one which he won't be expecting. But if you want me to leave right now, I will." He shrugged. "No hurt feelings."

Amanda said nothing for a moment. "I'm sorry," she finally said, her eyes watering. "When you tried to touch me—"

"I won't again," Jeff said. "Not without your permission." He paused. "Why did you want me to kiss you?"

"I don't know. I just . . . God, I'm messed up sometimes," Amanda confessed.

"Not your fault. I've been told that I am a fantastic kisser," Jeff said with a smile.

Despite herself Amanda smirked, a tear falling from her cheek. "Jeff—"

"I'll leave you alone," Jeff said, respectfully. "Goodnight, Amanda." He turned to leave.

"Just promise me one thing, Jeff," Amanda said. "When we see Gauis, I get to shoot him in the head."

That much was a promise he could easily make. "Okay," he nodded. "I promise."

* * *

The next morning he drove across the desert in a car he had been working on in the hotel. Even though the windows were cranked open, he could still feel perspiration running down his face. Gaius's camp was about an hour away by driving. By the time he got there, the sun would be setting, plummeting the temperature to freezing levels. The joy of living in a desert. "Are you ready for this?" he asked Amanda.

"Ready," she replied in the passenger's seat. Her hands were tightly bound.

Eventually they arrived at the compound, which used to be a naval base. Electrified wire ran around the length of the buildings. He didn't have a prayer of trying to get in undetected, but that wasn't in his plan. Jeff beeped his horn as he approached the gate. A group of people assembled before opening it. He was only able to take a step out of the car before one of Gaius's men searched him, and confiscated his gun. Another searched his car. As Jeff watched, the man roughly searched Amanda. Amanda, much to her credit, bore it in silence. Finally, the man searched the trunk and the dashboard, before finally closing the car door and letting out a loud whistle.

A minute later, Gaius stepped out of the compound. The slaver was in his late fifties, with gray hair mixed with white and a small beard. The man's age didn't make him any less dangerous—he wore a white, short-sleeved shirt, and Jeff could see bulging muscles and scars on his arms that would put most men to shame, especially in this day and age. The slaver's sharp, hazel eyes revealed little as he studied him closely, sizing him up.

"Well, well, isn't this a surprise," Gaius finally said. "Rumor has it you died at the hotel. I didn't expect to see you ever again."

In response, Jeff walked back to the car, opened the passenger door, and pulled out Amanda. "I ran into a few problems. Nothing I couldn't handle." He suddenly gripped Amanda's head with both hands, making her gasp. "I trust you will honor our arrangement. Or I'll snap her neck."

Gaius narrowed his eyes, sizing him up. "Goddamit. I underestimated you, kid. You don't play around."

"My daughter," Jeff stated. His heart started to beat faster in his chest. "Where is she?"

Gaius smirked. "I'm a man of my word." He gestured with his

hand towards a small, white shed to the left. Garbage littered the path, and spots of black mold decorated the walls.

Jeff roughly pushed Amanda into his arms, who stared at Gaius with loathing . . . and perhaps fear. He immediately turned and ran towards the shed. He couldn't help himself. He snarled in irritation as he realized the door was locked. "Jasmine!"

"One moment sir," one of Gaius's men said in amusement. He unlocked the door and grabbed the startled Jeff. Before he could react, he was shoved inside and the door closed behind him.

The stench hit Jeff as his eyes adjusted to the dim light from a lamp in the corner. He could see a sleeping bag nearby, almost completely covered except for a hint of brown hair. He stepped forwards and yanked the blanket away. A rotting skeleton stared back at him.

Howls of laughter came from outside.

* * *

Amanda heard a shriek come from the shed as the men around her roared with laughter, but she didn't have time to figure out what happened as Gaius gripped her by the waist.

"So, little one," he said, reeking of sweat and alcohol. "You thought it would be fun to sabotage my supply line." He took out an eight-inch knife. "I like to have fun too. If I'm feeling nice, I might even take it slow." He slowly lowered the knife down her body. "Come on, give us a kiss—"

Amanda didn't hesitate. She leaned forwards and bit him on the lip. *Hard.* Gaius howled in pain. "Gregory, now!"

Gregory dropped from a hidden compartment in the floor of the car, uzi in hand. He fired at the crowd of slavers before they could reach for their guns. Amanda felt her kidneys explode as Gaius punched her, his face glowing with rage and blood. She fell to her knees. Gaius lifted his fist again.

Jeff appeared out of nowhere, stopping the blow. He punched Gaius in the head. Enraged, the slaver swung his knife at Jeff. Looking surprisingly calm, Jeff dodged the blow, grabbed Gaius's hand, and slammed the knife back into his side. Without stopping, Jeff yanked the knife away and used it to free Amanda's bonds as the slaver fell to his knees.

Amanda glanced at Jeff in astonishment. By this time, Gregory had stopped shooting, and every other slaver lay dead. "Are you all right?" she asked Jeff.

Jeff nodded. "Yep."

Bemused, Amanda turned to the shed. The door was barely holding together by its hinges. "Was your daughter—"

"No," Jeff said. "He wanted me to think she was dead, but that wasn't her. She's around here somewhere, I know it." He glanced at Gaius, who was crawling in the dirt. "I kept him alive for you."

"Thank you," Amanda whispered, hugging him. She took a spare gun from Gregory and stepped towards the slaver, her face cold.

"Bitch," Gaius whispered, gripping his bloody side. "Don't you know who I am? Stupid—"

Amanda shot him in the head. She released a trembling breath, silent tears falling from her eyes. He was gone. Finally. Maybe now the nightmares could end.

"Now what?" Gregory asked.

Amanda opened her eyes and tossed away the gun "I'm tired of killing for today. And I have a feeling there are plenty of people here who want to be let out." She grinned as she saw a small eight-year-old girl in one of the cages, staring at Jeff and shaking. "Starting with that one."

The look on Jeff's face was priceless. "I could kiss you right now," he said to her.

Amanda grinned. "Go ahead."

COLLATERAL DAMAGE

David Murphy

Hartnett had come from Belfast to orchestrate a purge of three men, the known local wing of the splinter group that had split the Republican movement. "We take them at four tomorrow morning." He paused. "All three to be rounded up and brought to Noone's Field. Any questions?"

Noone's Field? My skin went clammy; my head felt light. Prisoners were interrogated there before their bodies were dumped.

At dismissal I avoided Hartnett's friends and enemies alike and walked quickly to the back of the farmhouse. I locked myself into the toilet. I leaned against the wall to prevent it closing in around me, and studied the list again.

It was an everyday name, Luke, chosen for brevity to sit beside Mulraney-Murphy. One followed the other in a harmonious way, the plain in tune with the convoluted. If only life were as simple. I balled the sheet and looked into the bowl. Someone had been here before me. I flushed the list around the bend into pipes and drains all over an ugly, stinking world. I needed a place and a time to think, so when the crumpled-up list had disappeared, I put the lid down and sat on it. I heard again the lament of a referee's final whistle. Luke had wheeled around to me that day when Cliftonville beat Linfield. Of all his friends he had chosen me, his *Da*, for his embrace. I saw again his shiny teenaged joy, and in an instant re-lived all the empty terraces I've stood on since, my Saturdays at Solitude, my head everywhere but on the Reds.

Approaching midnight, a young man peered into an alleyway. I whispered that syllable again, *Luke*, cooing it like I used to long ago. The breeze carried it to his ears. He froze.

"Hello, Luke." I stepped from behind a stack of bins, hands in my pockets trying to look casual.

"What do *you* want?"

I saw spittle sail straight at me. "They're on to you, Luke. They'll come for you tomorrow morning. You've got . . . "

"They'll come for me? You mean you'll come for me. You're one of them, you prick."

Wafts of old arguments slithered down the alley. "There's going to be raids in the morning. I don't know why you're on the list but . . . "

"Of course you know why."

"We've no time for a wee chat." The alley walls reminded me of that toilet cubicle. They hemmed me in. "You've got to get out of here."

"I'm going nowhere."

"Aye, well then I've got to arrest you."

He stared at me like a dumb fish, which was understandable considering I had just blown my cover.

I started to lift my right hand out of my coat when he did the unthinkable. The metal cuffs were peeping from my pocket when he reached into his jacket and pulled out a gun.

"Luke!" I tried to show that I only had cuffs—how could I have raised a gun to my own son? Taking my hand out was my second, almost fatal, mistake.

In the moment he pointed the muzzle, time slowed. Memories

swooped from places long ago. Ghosts of long-dead ravens winged through the alley, flocks of them, swirling and diving around my head, none as fast as the lean bullet cutting through their feathers, obliterating all memories as it tore into my arm.

No past tense then, only present. No pain, only a picture of Luke running away.

To my astonishment, two Police Service uniforms jumped him at the head of the alley. All three fell to the ground. The gun discharged again, pinging its load off the pavement into the grimy Ulster air. The uniforms had him, one yelling into his lapel for backup. Then the pain came. Seconds later I heard the wail of sirens before slumping to the ground, a useless pair of cuffs tangled around my blood-stained fingers as I tried to stem the flow from my arm.

* * *

From my hospital bed, I replayed over and over the memories that had flashed at me in the alley: kite-flying in the park, fishing in the stream, the joy of seeing him stay on his bike that Christmas long gone. I saw his angular face; his neck muscles straining in a police arm-lock as he spat me his last farewell, his eyes screamed: "what kind of father shops his own son?" I stared at the hospital ceiling, trying to get to grips with a son who shoots his own father. How was he to know that I hadn't set up those two uniforms to jump him? "Bit of a coincidence," he might add in his Queen's University accent, that they happened to be passing by the alley and heard the commotion.

Another uniform stood outside my ward to protect me from Hartnett and his cronies who were doubtless itching to get even with a traitor. This third uniform held the door open for a decorated officer to step inside. I nearly needed to ring the bell for a bedpan when I saw who it was.

"Well, Murphy, I believe the bullet went clean through?" The

Assistant Chief Constable offered me his hand, nodding at my arm.

I was so surprised by his chummy tone that I could not speak.

He smiled as he pulled up a chair. "Normally," he began, "we have no time for maverick, one-man operations. We try to discourage impulsive actions on the part of our officers, and our other agents. But given the record of the man who shot you, and that he was your son, and that you were trying to make an arrest, we have nothing but the highest praise for the way you tackled him."

I could hardly believe my ears. Luke's attempt to kill me, plus the cuffs in my blood-stained hand, had made me a hero in the eyes of the Service.

"Of course," the officer droned on, "there were witnesses on the street. Dozens of people saw you being taken away by ambulance. The IRA may now be aware that you've been working for us all along. They'll be after you. We took items from your flat this morning: clothing, footwear, a suitcase. These things, plus some money we'll give you, should tide you over for a month or so. The hospital says you'll be discharged tomorrow. In the morning, we'll escort you to the mainland. The process of permanent re-location takes a few weeks. There's a lot of paperwork involved: a new passport, credit cards, a new identity."

His words washed over me. I looked beyond his distinguished rank to walls of sickly green. Those walls had me surrounded; tilting over, top-heavy with the guilt of what I had been: snitch, mole, or the dread-word spoken in hushed tones by my own people, my ex-own people, *informer*. The colour of the walls mocked me, not with the green vomit of what I had been, but with what I had become: a snake in the supergrass, and what I would soon be: exiled, banished, Sinn Féiner no longer. A true Mé Féiner—*Myself Alone*—in every sense.

Three weeks later my request to visit Luke was sanctioned. Such a cold word: "sanctioned," it rhymes with the hollow sound of clanging gates. The final sharp metallic clink stays with me always. It brought us face to face.

"Thanks for seeing me, Luke. I know it's not easy. There are things I need to explain, things you should know."

I found myself wishing for a glass of water. My prepared speech was in smithereens. One look at his face morphing from adult to teenage to wain made my brain tumble through fifteen years to a day when rumours had flown across Luke's schoolyard that a man had died in the local factory. After he had ran home, mum told him that, yes, a man had died but not to worry, it wasn't *Da*. Later that night, she had joked with me about how worried young Luke had looked. That had been in the days when I was the Best Da in the World. Back then things righted themselves instantly for a nine-year old. How I wished for simple solutions now. His face was adult again, glacial.

"Have they fixed you up with a new life?"

"Aye." I struggled to meet his gaze.

"Where are you staying? England?"

I nodded.

"Devon? Cornwall?"

"You know I can't answer that."

"Did they escort you here?"

"They offered, but I made my own way." I tried to make it sound like an everyday thing.

"Did you switch to a local bus once you crossed the border?"

"I'm not answering that." I swallowed. Something about his chatty demeanour did not ring true.

"Will you go back the same way?"

"Listen, Lu—"

"The beard won't help. They'll expect that, and the dyed hair. Where will they send you permanently? Down under? New Zealand?"

183

"Luke, I—"

"You bastard!" He was off his seat, eyes bulging so close to the glass his breath clouded over the snarl on his mouth. He tried to punch me through the panel. I reeled back in shock. In the instant his fist bounced off glass, his expression changed from anger to pain. For a moment he was my small boy again, hurt from a very cruel game of make-believe.

I held my hand up to indicate to closed circuit that I could handle it. "I saved your life and what thanks did I get? You shot your own father!" I hoped that deep down I could draw the bitterness and resentment from him. A faint hope. He stood with his back to me, hunching over his bruised fist.

"Hartnett was going to round you up, you and two others. They would've tortured and shot you. I had only a few hours to figure out what to do. I tried to get you to run, but you wouldn't! The only way I could save you was by turning you in. Did you really think your Da was taking out a gun? Those were handcuffs in my pocket, not a . . . "

"Where did you get the cuffs?" he snorted as he turned. "The local station or do you use them for bondage with that whore?"

That startled me. Politics was bad enough without bringing *her* up. "That's not fair. I'm sorry things didn't work out between your mother and I. We all make mistakes."

"Mistakes? You betrayed my mother. Then you betrayed your country. And all you can say is: 'we all make mistakes'? You're only a cunt."

"Shut up and listen. Your mother and I had our difficulties, especially after they recruited you . . . " My voice broke at what he had turned his education to, how he had swallowed their rhetoric, turning his technical expertise to carry out their orders.

"Will you be bringing her with you, the whore?" His callous

eyes made me look at the hard floor. "Answer me one thing before you go," he said coldly. "When did you go over to the Brits?"

"After your mother and I divorced, around the time I realised the carnage you'd been responsible for. That really put the hat on it." I studied him hard. He did not react. "One day I had enough. I rang the confidential hotline. And didn't I do the right thing? Didn't I what! Aye, three weeks ago they expected me to sacrifice you! Maybe involving me in that was some kind of mistake. Maybe they didn't twig that the Murphy part of your name is mine, but I doubt it." I paused and drew breath. "The police set up a meeting. They gave me more money than the factory ever paid. As for the woman you called a whore . . . " I looked at him directly. "She and I split up a year after I left your mother. I have no one now. You're all I've got."

It was a plea that drew one last accusing glare. I knew then that he was right. It was time to go. There was nothing left, and nothing left to say. All the years of rearing him had come to this. This time he had no gun to pull so I took something from my pocket again. I held up a piece of paper and showed him the lines written on it. I gave him a wee minute to memorise them.

I went back the way I came: a bus down South. I stepped on the streets of Dublin and turned up my collar against the cold. A woolly hat blended me into the background. I walked the streets, shoulder-rubbing Southerners who felt safe, for the moment, from their history. I told myself there could never be reconciliation—he had called his father a cunt, after all. I hoped that maybe, just maybe, he had aimed deliberately for my arm.

It was time for the flight to my temporary safe-house in England. I looked out at shades of green slipping by beyond the wings. When he is released, through breakout or under whatever new agreement, I know he will seek me out. They say there is no more determined and dangerous freedom fighter than an educated one. I ought to know. I reared one.

As he sits alone in his prison cell, with these fields of green falling far away from me, I hope he remembers the address in Argentina that I held up to the glass panel for him to memorise, that he will regard it as the calling card I intended it to be. Whether he reads it as, *Come to Me, Luke* or *Come and Get Me, Luke* I will leave entirely up to him.

Article Six, Paragraph Two

Robert J. Santa

"I am hot," Miller said as he wiped his forehead with his sleeve. "I can't believe they scheduled a war for August."

"Maybe you could run for office," said Jancowicz. "Then you could put them all in the springtime."

"I like the springtime."

"October?"

Miller considered for a moment.

"I guess summer's not too bad," he finally said. "It's already miserable. Might as well have a war, too."

"We're glad you approve."

"Incoming!" Dakota Tom had time to give the warning or to dive for cover but not both. Miller and Jancowicz hit the ground as flame and noise and pieces of Dakota Tom exploded all around them.

"I'm hit," Jancowicz said quite matter-of-factly. Miller looked over and saw what appeared to be a compound fracture of the left tibia. Then he pulled a section of Dakota Tom's forearm out of Jancowicz's calf, stared in horror at it, and tossed it aside. Jancowicz only shrugged.

"Guess I'm not," he said.

"Technically," said Miller, "it still qualifies you for a Purple Heart."

Jancowicz harrumphed.

"If I got a Purple Heart," he said sternly, "for every scratch I ever got in combat, my uniform would be too heavy to lift." Jancowicz flipped the actuator on his rifle then quickly stuck his head up over the top of the wall, pulling it back just as quickly. He waited a moment then stood up as he fired over the top of the wall. Less than a second after he dropped back down, several shots ricocheted off the stone above him.

"How many?" Miller asked.

"A lot," Jancowicz replied. "There's four or five dug in by that cluster of stumps. I saw two running right. There were two at twelve o'clock, about forty meters out. Now there's only one."

Several bursts of gunfire ripped into their barricade, and both men knew it was cover fire.

"How far to that tree cluster again?" asked Miller.

"Sixty-two to the front edge. Call it sixty-five."

Miller dialed in the distance and dropped a round into the mortar. He followed the gun's immediate coughing with another shell then readied his rifle. When the first explosion sounded in the near distance, he stood and opened full automatic fire to his right. Before the second shell landed, he adjusted his aim and cut down someone who was advancing. He dropped back into the hole. Jancowicz stood and fired a short burst then crouched.

"What did you see?" he asked over more impacts above him.

"No one at twelve," said Miller. "Couldn't see anything on the right other than the one I hit. Didn't get a look at the stumps."

"I'm getting ready to advance to the rear."

"I'm with you, Sarge."

An explosion behind them was very close, perhaps twenty meters back, and they covered as dirt and bits of debris struck their backs and heads. They stood as they were still being pelted. Jancowicz fired to the right and Miller to the left. When Miller ducked, Jancowicz was still firing. He spoke, still standing.

"I think that's all of them," he said. Miller also stood and swept his rifle barrel slowly across the terrain. Nobody shot at them.

"I'll be damned," Miller finally said. He looked around again. "So where did that shell come from?"

Another blast of flame and noise came from behind them, closer than the last time. They both felt the pressure push them against the wall as they fell back down and tried for some kind of cover.

"Advance on three," Jancowicz shouted over the ringing in his ears. Miller nodded. "One, two, three."

They launched themselves out of their hole, scrambling around the wall. They ran forward and fired bursts ahead of them into the smoke and shadows. Forty meters went by in a blur of noise and gray. Both of them slid behind another wall. Miller looked at Jancowicz and saw a mirror image of himself: sweat, dirt, and confusion.

"Anyone shooting at us?" he asked.

"I didn't get hit," said Jancowicz. "You?"

"Nope."

"We need to find that mortar."

"That's a ten-four, Sarge." Miller looked down at Jancowicz's rifle. There was a tiny green light flashing near the gun sight. Miller saw the light on his own rifle was also flashing.

"Stand down, Sergeant," he said.

An explosion rocked the ground halfway between where the two of them lay and the hole they had come from.

"You must be joking," Jancowicz said, knowing full well that Miller wasn't.

"Let's find a way out of here." Miller raised himself into a crouch and surveyed the rubble around him. A gunshot resounded as a bullet impacted the stones several feet away. Miller ducked back down.

"That was a pistol shot," said Jancowicz. "I figure that guy on the mortar is all by himself, and if he had a rifle or something heavier, he would be using it. We can charge him, laying down cover fire."

"We can do no such thing, Sergeant," Miller said, his voice becoming firmer. "We've reached our limit. All we can do is get our butts out of here."

"That's nuts."

"That's the law."

A shell landed, wide of their position by a good twenty yards. But it was on their line.

"He's got our range," Miller said. "Let's get out of here."

They sprinted in the direction opposite the last blast. Jancowicz held the trigger down on his rifle and let automatic fire chatter out ahead of them. Miller ran with his rifle quiet in his hands. A low building that had its roof blown away gave them refuge.

"Can't stay here," Jancowicz said between breaths as he popped the magazine out of his weapon and replaced it with a fresh one. "Too big a target."

"Stow that magazine," said Miller, but Jancowicz clicked it in and pulled back the slide on his rifle.

"Stuff it," he said.

"That's an order, Sergeant."

"Then stuff it, sir," Jancowicz replied. Before Miller could say anything else, he continued. "That guy's trying to kill us. I'm not going to make it easy for him."

"You could accidentally hit him."

"I won't cry myself to sleep at night if I do."

"That's a violation of the War Convention," said Miller. Then the far corner of the building disappeared in a thunder of yellow and white light. Very little of the debris reached them.

"Less talking," Jancowicz said as he stood back up, "more running." He stepped into the doorway and dove back inside when a hail of automatic fire chewed up the wall beside him.

"Mortar guy's got some friends," Miller said.

"I noticed," Jancowicz said from the floor. "Got a problem over here, Lieutenant."

Miller dropped to his knees as he set his rifle down. He helped Jancowicz turn over and saw the blood on his forearm.

"It doesn't feel too bad," said Jancowicz as he sat up. Miller took out his knife and cut the uniform where the bullet hole was. A round had passed through the meat of the sergeant's forearm a few centimeters below the elbow.

"Lucky," Miller said as he opened the seal on a field patch.

"Yeah," Jancowicz said. "I feel real lucky." He drew in his breath sharply as Miller pressed the dressing onto his arm and wrapped it tightly.

Another explosion roared, and while it was not a hit, the building still shook. Dust settled down onto them from the walls.

"We can't stay here, either," said Jancowicz as Miller tied the bandage into a tight knot.

"I don't see an option other than surrender," Miller said.

"No, thanks. I spent fourteen months sitting out the last one in a POW camp. Not the best time I ever had."

"What else can we do?"

"We can fight our way out," Jancowicz suggested.

"And bluff? Firing into the air is just going to get us killed."

"I won't be bluffing."

Miller fixed him with a steady stare.

"We're maxed out, Sergeant," he said without taking his eyes from Jancowicz. "That's what those lights are for, to keep us from taking more lives than is arranged."

"Then the boys with the big brains should have disabled these guns instead of putting pretty lights on them."

"You know as well as I do that's a stupid thing to do to a soldier in the wild." Miller stopped and stared Jancowicz in the eyes. "We're going to surrender by the book."

"I didn't bring a hankie," Jancowicz said.

"We'll show our flashers." As Miller reached for his rifle, Jancowicz picked up his and brought its barrel crashing down. Both weapons clattered together with tiny breaking sounds. When he lifted his rifle again, Jancowicz saw the plastic bulb was broken on Miller's as well.

Miller picked up his rifle and examined it for only a second. His face flushed almost purple.

"Oops," Jancowicz said, rising to his feet.

"Tampering with a weapon is a violation of Convention," Miller said through clenched teeth.

"Sorry, Lieutenant. This is war. Accidents happen." Jancowicz moved beside the doorway and stood pressed against the wall. He put just his rifle out in the open and held the trigger down, pouring automatic fire outside. When he ejected the magazine and replaced it, he looked back at Miller.

Miller had his sidearm out. It was pointed at Jancowicz's head. The tiny green light that pulsed behind the gunsight only emphasized the size of the barrel.

"Drop the weapon, Sergeant," said Miller.

"Can't do that, sir. It's not part of my training." He peeked around the corner and pulled his head back. A few dozen bullets slammed into the doorway and the wall. The instant they stopped,

Jancowicz aimed and fired a long burst.

"That was probably a violation, too," he said as he ducked back behind cover. "On the plus side, there's one less guy trying to kill us."

"You did *not* accrue another loss," Miller said as he lowered his pistol. It was half question and half statement.

"I love the way you college boys talk. Yeah, I got one."

"That's over the limit."

"I know," Jancowicz said. He stepped out and fired another short burst. When he looked back, he saw that Miller had re-raised his pistol.

"Drop the weapon, Sergeant," repeated Miller, and Jancowicz heard the deadliness in his voice.

Jancowicz hesitated. Without warning, Miller disappeared in a cloud of fire and noise. Jancowicz instinctively threw himself aside, but the blast pushed him and rolled him across the floor. He was disoriented for only a moment. When his head cleared, the majority of Miller's shattered body was directly before him.

Running footsteps sounded outside. Jancowicz lifted his rifle as someone appeared in the doorway firing into the room well over his prone body. Jancowicz squeezed the trigger and released it, letting out only a short burst. All five bullets struck the silhouette, which jerked spasmodically and fell down backward with arms and legs splayed. Another soldier charged through the doorway, rifle on automatic, and Jancowicz fired into him as well. He fell inside the room and flopped only once before lying still.

He never saw the soldier in the window and was dead without hearing the burst that tore open his chest and skull. Jancowicz's rifle clattered onto the stone floor as two more soldiers entered the building and looked around.

"We're all clear, Captain," said one of them. The captain was just outside the doorway, waving his arms over his head to someone in the distance who packed up his mortar and began jogging toward them.

"Give us a minute, please," said the sergeant in the window, and the two soldiers in the building went outside. The sergeant joined the captain who had walked inside and stood over the body of Sergeant Jancowicz.

"I can't say I'm comfortable with this," the sergeant said.

"We never would have been able to advance," replied the captain as he looked down, "with them dug in here the way they were."

"Oh, I understand," said the sergeant. "I'm just saying I'm not comfortable, is all."

"Noted," the captain said. "Call support and have these bodies recovered."

"Yes, sir." The sergeant picked up his radio and spoke into it.

The captain turned away from Jancowicz's body and walked over to his fallen men. He picked up both of their rifles and pulled the tape from their barrels. He laid them back down beside the soldiers and stared at the flashing lights. Then he walked out of the building.

WORKER

Jason Lairamore

America was in need of a miracle.

"Thank you for coming," Dr. Murphy, neurosurgeon, said to his fellow surgeons. "Our grand experiment is a go."

Dr. Richie and Dr. Smith, both young orthopedics, nodded, their eagerness obvious.

Dr. Samms, GI specialist, and Dr. Kingly, world-famous cardiovascular surgeon, both older men, frowned.

"You've found funding?" Dr. Samms asked.

"Senator McGowin is backing us," Dr. Murphy replied.

Dr. Samms smiled. "And who his backing him?"

"President Cole."

Dr. Samms lost his smile.

"You've got his money?" Dr. Kingly asked. Dr. Murphy nodded.

Dr. Samms shook his head. "The effects on humans are unknown. Animal studies aren't enough."

"We're as ready as we're going to be," Dr. Murphy said. "Something has to be done."

Dr. Samms nodded.

"What of candidates?" Dr. Kingly asked.

"There is one right here in the Raleigh area. He could undergo the procedures today, if need be."

"And you've got his consent?" Dr. Kingly followed.

"Not yet, but I will. The man is a worker, the real deal."

* * *

It was Sunday, and I was sitting in Dr. Murphy's outreach clinic. The waiting room smelt of mildew. The sick, tired, and lazy sat about waiting for antibiotics and disability assessments. The water stain in the ceiling over the entryway had grown since last week. That really bugged me.

Ever since the icecaps had melted, the world had gone to hell.

The pamphlets on the coffee table were dated 2065 and labeled, *TISSUE ENGINEERING: A WAY TO BEAT THE EFFECTS OF AGING.* That sounded pretty good. Too bad nobody but the rich had the money to afford the treatments.

The only good thing about tissue engineering was that I was a universal donor. There were just a handful of people like me in the Raleigh area. I got paid to give samples. That was the only reason I sat there with the masses in the stinky waiting room on my only day off work.

"Wesley Chaynes, Room 2," said the tired-looking receptionist.

"Get my money ready," I called as I headed toward the procedure room. It wouldn't take Dr. Murphy long to excise whatever piece of me he needed for his grow tubes.

I changed from my sleeveless, denim shirt and blue jeans into a hospital gown then lay down on the room's cold steel table.

"Morning, Doc," I said as he entered. "When are you going to fix that stain in the ceiling out front?" I asked him the same thing every week. He had yet to answer.

Dr. Murphy's eyes were riveted to his pad. He always reminded me of what a mad scientist ought to look like. It was something in his eyes that did the trick.

"Tenth biopsy," he said. He was probably right. I hadn't counted. "You still working?" he asked, like he didn't already know the answer.

"Always," I said. I was one of the few. Unemployment was up to over forty percent in the country. Laziness begot laziness.

Dr. Murphy didn't ask any more questions. He drew a vial of blood from my elbow and packed it away for transport to who knew where.

"How would you like to be four times as strong, Mr. Chaynes?" he asked.

I sat up on the table's edge and shrugged. "I'd like a lot of things, Doc."

His eyes were looking extra crazy. "Would you like to never get tired, to need no sleep, to require hardly any food?"

I stood and changed back into my clothes.

"What do you want, Doc?"

"You'd make a good candidate for our newest program," he said.

I huffed. "All the old government programs worked so well."

"It's two months," Dr. Murphy said. "Two months that pays a year's worth of factory wages."

That got my attention.

"You cover the time off from work?" I asked.

"Everything will be taken care of."

"What's it called?"

"The Labor Specialization Program."

"Risk factors?" I asked.

"It's experimental."

"So, I could die?"

Dr. Murphy paused. "Doubtful," he finally said.

I'd already decided back when he'd told me about the money.

"Where do I sign?"

Dr. Murphy fiddled with his pad for a few then handed me an e-pen. I signed on the dotted line and a little piece of paper cycled out of his machine.

"Procedure will occur in the morning," he said.

I looked at the piece of paper. It had an address on it.

"That fast?" I asked.

"That fast," he said.

* * *

Even on Sunday morning the streets of Wake Forrest were crowded. I dodged around the mass of milling people and water puddles and walked from the clinic to the bus stop. People mostly kept their hands to themselves. Inadequate sewer systems, a messed-up climate, worldwide famine, it all had raised infection rates to new highs.

The bus took me from Wake Forrest to the suburb of Sunnyside. From there I walked down Allen Street. Home was a fifth floor, one bedroom apartment in a dilapidated building. I climbed the stairs since the elevator was out. At the top I had to wait a minute to catch my breath before continuing down the hallway.

Helen sat on the couch watching television. She was just as I'd left her when I'd gone to the clinic. It always surprised me to see how much she'd changed in the ten years since we'd gotten married. I was the one working twelve hours days. She just sat at home. If anyone should be showing their age, it'd have been me. But to look at her you'd think she was fifty instead of thirty-two.

"Morning hon," I called as I shut the door.

She didn't answer. She never moved from looking at the television. I walked up behind her and kissed the top of her head. Her brown hair was thinning and left a greasy sheen to my lips. She didn't acknowledge the kiss. I walked to the kitchenette.

A little water and a quick nuke in the microwave transformed the powder in my bowl to a mush that was supposed to taste like beef and oats. I ate in the near silence of a talk show while looking out the little window over the sink.

After wiping my plastic bowl with an antibiotic napkin and putting it back in the cupboard, I leaned against the cabinet and faced the back of Helen's head.

"I signed up for one of the new government programs today."

A chuckle came from her, but she didn't turn from the show.

"It's supposed to make me stronger, need less sleep. I could work more and make us enough money to move out of this dump."

She cackled.

"I'd like to improve our situation, hon, make things better."

She shook her head.

"Doc said I'd be gone two months. You alright with that? Money will be in the account. All you'll have to do is go get food when you need it."

"Okay," she said. I thought about walking up and turning the television off, but didn't. She'd just get mad.

* * *

Dr. Murphy arrived early at the research surgical center, but he hadn't beaten Mr. Chaynes.

"Good morning," Dr. Murphy said.

"Good as we get," Mr. Chaynes replied.

Dr. Murphy opened the door to the clinic and led the way to his office. He offered Mr. Chaynes a chair, which he refused.

"Mrs. Finley from legal will be here soon," Dr. Murphy said.

"Tell me more about the procedure."

"It's invasive," Dr. Murphy said. "Most of your major systems will be affected. Muscle, bone, digestive, heart, nervous system."

"What's the chance something could go wrong?"

"Nothing will go wrong, Mr. Chaynes, but if it does your wife will be taken care of."

Mr. Chaynes nodded then stuck out his hand. He had large knuckles and fingers twice as thick as Dr. Murphy's. His palms were rough, like shoe leather. Dr. Murphy shook.

"Man to man," Mr. Chaynes said. "I hold you responsible." Dr. Murphy nodded and smiled. There was a knock on the office door. Mrs. Finley had arrived.

While Mr. Chaynes worked on signing all the papers the state and national government required, the two orthopedic surgeons and their teams arrived. Dr. Murphy watched them set up their various equipment and tools through the operating room observation glass. The procedure called for total joint replacements for all extremities, including rod placement down bone shafts. There were also the bionic hands and feet that the two orthopods had developed. Those were a real marvel.

Mr. Chaynes came from Mrs. Finley's office a little glassy-eyed a few minutes later. She led him down the hall to the surgical prep room and quietly handed Dr. Murphy a folder.

"You're not touching my brain, doc," Mr. Chaynes said.

Dr. Murphy nodded and Mrs. Finley walked away. He quickly scanned the printout Mrs. Finley had handed him. Mr. Chaynes had signed off on all the experimental specifics except the brain enhancement.

"Have you any more questions, Mr. Chaynes?"

Mr. Chaynes shook his head.

"Then good luck." He left and went to the orthopedic observation deck.

"All procedures," he said through the intercom to the two

orthopedics. "He's in Room 1."

* * *

Sounds of drilling and hammering carried from the operating room. Dr. Murphy sat and watched. Dr. Samms entered.

"Hope you picked a winner," Dr. Samms said. He set down a silver suitcase and sat beside Dr. Murphy.

Dr. Murphy handed over the printout and eyed the suitcase. Inside rested the synthetic digestive system specified for Mr. Chaynes' biology. Like the hands and feet of the orthopedic surgeons, Dr. Samms' synthetic system, a replacement for the small intestine, was a prototype.

"We've done years of planning, have spent countless hours in research and development," Dr. Murphy said. "We're past hope. We need this to work."

Dr. Samms sighed and rubbed at his neck while he read the report.

"It will work," the old doctor said. "What worries me is President Cole's sudden interest and backing."

"He wants to win an election. I don't care his reasons. It needs done regardless of the politics."

"You'll find no argument from me."

Dr. Kingly entered a few minutes later carrying a suitcase of his own. His work in heart and circulatory arrays was near magical.

"Dr. Kingly," Dr. Murphy nodded.

"Are we ready?"

"As ready as we are ever going to be."

* * *

Mr. Chaynes lay hidden beneath a mass of cryogenic machines, pulsating pressure cuffs, blood circulating tubes, and stiff, plastic blue paper. The Orthos assisted the others in bringing in a multitude of

201

covered tubs, machines, and preparation tables to be used on the next series of surgeries. Dr. Zimmer, anesthesiologist, sat at his post at Mr. Chaynes' head, working his single machine and checking the flow of medicines going through the patient's central line.

Mr. Chaynes had already received more traumatic surgery than history could claim and the process had only just begun.

Without a word the three surgeons went to work; Dr. Samms on Mr. Chaynes' right, Dr. Kingly on his left, and Dr. Murphy underneath, in a tight recess built specifically for this surgery. The table on which Mr. Chaynes lay possessed a three-inch gap running from the base of the skull to just below the coccyx. Dr. Murphy would have to work like an auto mechanic changing oil while he performed his delicate neurological work. It was a good thing he was wearing a full body surgical suit. Gravity would not be his friend as Mr. Chaynes' blood fell to the floor.

* * *

I woke more sore than I'd thought I could ever be. It wasn't pain. I couldn't call it pain. The soreness broke itself into individual parts so small that it jarred my mind with the specific multiplicity of it all. I'd felt crazy soreness before, or thought I had. Working seven straight doubles hard labor could make my body ache in places I hadn't known existed. This was something different. I felt new stuff. And it was all sore. The doctors must have given me some good meds. This couldn't be real.

It took me by surprise that my eyes were open. Vision broke in among the soreness like a weed in a hand-made rock walkway. I lay on a bed. My entire body was covered in bandages. Tubes and wires came out in various spots. Machines beeped nearby.

Dr. Murphy stood at my bedside. "Doc," I said. Even my voice was sore.

"You're awake," the good doctor observed.

"Good of you to notice."

I lost sight of the doc as he walked away.

"But, you've just been brought to recovery. Those meds . . . " I heard him open his phone and hit a few numbers.

"Dr. Zimmer, get down here."

* * *

Two days passed. President Cole and his staff, along with Senator McGowin and his staff, sat on the front row of R&D's conference hall. They waited for Dr. Murphy to begin his presentation.

Dr. Murphy posted Mr. Chaynes' base values then listed the specifics for the various surgical procedures. Next he showed them the forecasted seven-day estimates and overlay that with Mr. Chaynes' actual data.

Things were progressing too fast. This was the stuff of fairy tales.

The aides to the president and senator began whispering to their respective politician.

They asked questions, thanked him for his answers, and jotted down notes. He updated them on new projection data and stated his own amazement at Mr. Chaynes' progress.

President Christopher Cole sat reclined in his chair staring at Dr. Murphy while his aides typed furiously on their pads.

His voice was a southern drawl that went well with his out-thrust jaw and tan complexion.

"Seems like you're missin' an important component in your testing, Doctor."

Dr. Murphy raised his eyebrows to better invite the question. President Cole smiled that disarming smile that had won him his last election.

"X-ray's better than good, strength is off the charts, as is stamina, he's sleepin' less than an elf on Christmas Eve and can do everything you put him through eatin' a peanut a day."

"Mr. President, the data is much more detailed than that."

"I know, son, I know. You boys have been hard at it and have jumped every hoop with bells a'ringin'. What I've been sitting here thinkin', though is what do you think is going through that boy's head?"

"Sir?"

"Hellfire, doctor, the boy's not even human anymore, not after all that work."

One of the aides handed the president a sheet of paper.

"A mechanical heart with a 240 ml stroke volume, a resting heart rate of 35 BPM, and the best arteries regeneration science could produce are all involved in pumping blood through his system at twice the efficiency of a marathon runner."

"Well, yes."

"His digestive system is getting 500 percent more nutritional value from ingested food. And you have no idea the effects that might have on everything else."

"There is much stipulation on future studies."

"Dr. Murphy, you didn't touch the brain, per patient specs, but you did work on the peripheral nerves, bar none. Given all those changes, that brain of his has a lot to accommodate to."

"Yes sir, it does. Not to mention the extensive trauma associated with all the orthopedic surgery."

The President shook his head. "Then why haven't you got a psychiatrist on hand?"

"The original model didn't call in psychology until week four."

"Better upgrade that. Think about it, you get that boy angry, he could kill you on accident by poking you in the chest."

"Uh . . . " Dr. Murphy was at a loss. The possibility hadn't occurred to him.

"America needs more productive workers," the President said. "Ones that don't mind high tax rates and heavy, body-wrenching labor. That's gonna take some psychology assessment, no matter what you do to his body."

"Yes sir, right away, sir."

* * *

I lay back on the soft vinyl fabric of the bench press and grabbed the bar. The weight was something from a dream. It reminded me of re-runs from the world's strongest man television show. I used to watch that show with Dad when I was a kid. Five hundred pounds rested there, slightly bending the metal bar, and I was to do ten reps. I doubted a car engine weighed that much.

When I gave my first tentative push, the bar nearly sprung from my hands. Each rep sang to and from my chest as easy as breathing.

I did an extra couple of reps, just because it felt so good, then racked the bar and sat. Dr. Murphy stood there with his pad. His eyes seemed to get bigger day by day. Gone was his evil scientist twinkle. It had been replaced by a look of surprise.

I nodded toward the weight at my back. "So what does that prove?"

"It p-p-proves . . . " Good Doctor Murphy was developing a stammer as well. "It proves you're strong."

I shook my head.

"I used to work with a great, big guy named Old Mike," I said. "Old Mike looked like a bear wearing a shirt. He used to change semi trailer tires by hand when there was a perfectly good lift not ten feet away. I always thought the guy was about as smart as a brick."

"Why's that?" Dr. Murphy asked.

I shrugged. "Why waste the energy when there was a tool that could help you do it just as fast and a lot safer?"

Dr. Murphy typed something on his pad.

"When can I get out of here, doc?"

"Soon." He always said that. "How about let's strap on some ten pound ankle weights and run an hour on the treadmill at seven miles per hour and max incline?"

Boring stuff. He might as well tell me to go stand in a corner and stare at the wall.

"Got a web pad I can peruse during?"

Doctor Murphy's mouth hung open for just a moment before snapping shut. Then he sported that surprised look again.

"Uh, sure, Mr. Chaynes. I'll bring you one from the library."

* * *

Dr. Murphy sat in his office. President Cole was in front of him via video-link. The screen made the President's face larger than life.

"Mr. President, why have I been unable to reach the other doctors associated with the project?"

"Their part is complete," the president said. "This being a top-secret government experiment, there is no need for their continual involvement. They've got their nondisclosures all signed and are back to work at their various places of employ. You, Dr. Murphy, are still active and won't be able to reach them until your work is done. And then you will be greatly restricted by your nondisclosure agreement."

Dr. Murphy stared at him. President Cole stared back.

"We're after the same thing, doctor," the President said. "You just let me deal with how it gets implemented."

Dr. Murphy shook his head, confused at the sudden application of secrecy.

"How's our guinea pig?" the president asked.

"We're seven days out. Strength is at 412% baseline and

continues to climb. Cardiovascular fitness values have surpassed machine limits. Dietary—well, it doesn't matter what is ingested, it's completely absorbed. Neurological testing, eyesight, hearing, smell . . . " He shook his head. "We have no frame of reference upon which to test any of it. There is no way of testing his perceptual ability."

President Cole sighed. "I'm curious about the psych tests."

"The report," Dr. Murphy began.

"Is a waste of good electronic paper," the President finished. "I've talked to the therapist."

"His subjective opinion must not be allowed to jade the scientific study."

"Our boy scared the tester half to death."

"Mr. Chaynes is changing. He needs time."

"Doctor Murphy, Mr. Chaynes is an unknown and gettin' more so as we sit here and jabber. A college educated man, a specialist in human behavior and psychology, told me, with fear tremblin' his every word, that the subject's intelligence and capability bordered on precognition, that his very existence broke free of the human condition. I don't even know what that means."

"Sir . . . "

"Do the required brain surgery as outlined in your plan."

"That's an elective procedure, sir. All the procedures were elective."

"And I elect it, doctor." He gave Dr. Murphy that disarming smile seen on televisions across the globe.

"Mr. Chaynes has his rights."

"Do it."

"Find somebody else."

"I will," the President said.

The screen went black.

* * *

Work at the factory hummed around me, always singing, always waiting to be completed. There was no end. The line always ran thick with products to package, to paint, to screw, weld, and bolt. The break bell every two hours was but a bitter pause to the sweet monotony. Breaks were a waste of time.

I grabbed a snack every once in a while from one of the vending machines and took a shower in the employee lounge when my smell became an issue. But always the work beckoned. It wanted to be done. I could almost hear its plea.

I bought a chocolate bar and munched on it as I leaned against the doorframe that led to the factory floor. I feasted on the view of the various assembly lines. I'd worked them all, from assembly to shipping, from maintenance to quality control.

Someone tapped me on the shoulder. It was probably the foreman again, telling me it was time to take a shower. He was the only one that ever talked to me now. I guess that was okay. I could handle it for as long as it needed handling. I assured myself that it wouldn't be forever.

One of the old timers, a blue hair, eyed me while he chewed some gum. He wore bib overalls and a red flannel shirt rolled up to the elbow. His clothes were about as threadbare as mine, though his were more from actual age than from nonstop wear and tear.

I took another bite of chocolate.

"What'd they do to you, son?" he asked.

"I was lucky. I'm a universal donor."

"Lucky?" His frown had some deep lines in it. "You hear what the others are saying about you?"

I gave him a slow smile. "Don't worry. I ain't old Mike." It was as close as I could come to telling him the truth. I couldn't let my secret out. Not yet. America's miracle was too close to coming true.

The old man shook his head. The bell to return to work sounded. I chuckled and turned away. Work was calling and I was ready. I would always be ready.

* * *

Dr. Murphy had signed President Cole's nondisclosure form and had lived by it to the letter. He'd kept his nose out of it and had spoken to no one regarding the experiment.

The little old receptionist from the front poked her head in his office.

"Senator McGowin is here asking for you."

"Thank you. Please show him in."

"Can you explain this proposed surgical note to me?" Senator McGowin asked without preamble as he set foot in Dr. Murphy's office. The Senator was leafing through a folder he'd brought with him.

"I've already described my surgery to your surgeons, senator. Why are you really here?"

The senator tossed the thick folder down on the desk and crossed his arms.

"It's just . . . " He chewed on his lip. "Dr. Samms provided an amazing invention that is easy to replicate, as did Dr. Kingly and the two young Ortho-pods. But yours, Dr. Murphy, is a precision surgery that worries our surgeons."

"So what? Are the results to Mr. Chaynes not to your liking? I assume you performed all my experimental procedures, even the more invasive ones meant only for the severely mentally handicapped."

Senator McGowin nodded. "Yes. Our surgeons did them all. They did stuff to make Mr. Chaynes happy all the time and disconnected his ability for abstraction."

Dr. Murphy shook his head. *Abstract thought leads to loss of work production.* What a ridiculous concept.

They were monsters.

"What do you want, senator?"

"We'd like you on board, to help make sure our surgeons are doing it right."

"Not a chance." It was awful what they'd done to Mr. Chaynes. He'd shaken the man's hand in confidence, for God's sake.

The senator sighed. "I told them you'd say as much, but they wanted to be sure. Time is of the essence and all."

"President Cole's upcoming re-election."

The senator nodded. "We need more workers," he said. "We've already begun replicating the procedures to target groups. The more the better."

Dr. Murphy knew his shock leaked through, even though he tried to hold it back. President Cole planned to turn the entire country into one, big, non-thinking voter block.

"How is Mr. Chaynes?" he asked to cover his dismay.

"He's doing exactly as he is supposed to be doing," the senator replied with a smile.

Dr. Murphy didn't know what else to say. It wasn't like he could blow the lid on the whole mess. Nobody would believe him. His voice would be silenced before he even tried to go public. He had no illusions that they weren't keeping him under surveillance.

"Well," Senator McGowin said, picking up the folder. "Are you sure you won't reconsider?"

"No," he said. They couldn't force him to perform like they'd forced Mr. Chaynes. He opened his office door.

Senator McGowin took the hint. Dr. Murphy followed him to the waiting room, which was packed with the sick, the tired, and the lazy. Four men from the secret service stood in strategic places.

"Thank you for stopping by, senator."

"Yes, it looks like you've got your hands full."

He nodded and watched the senator leave. After he'd gone, Dr. Murphy walked to the receptionist desk.

"Who changed the ceiling tiles?" he asked. "What happened to the stain?"

The receptionist glanced at the ceiling then back to him.

"What stain?"

He only knew about it because Mr. Chaynes had made a point of mentioning it every time he visited.

"Huh, somebody must have finally fixed it, I guess," he muttered and went back to his office.

* * *

Yes, I fixed the tiles. Maybe Dr. Murphy will realize it was me and figure out that the brain surgery, for whatever reason, didn't take. Maybe he will feel better knowing that I'm fully functioning and improving every day. Maybe the others undergoing the surgery across the country will know to keep their traps shut so that the government continues to think it has everything under its control. That's a lot of maybes, I know, but it is what it is.

In the meantime, I will watch my back, and I will work. I am, after all, a worker.

One Last Risk

Latorial Faison

"And the day came when the risk to remain tight in a bud was more painful than the risk it took to blossom."
-Anais Nin

It was an August morning that none of us had awaited. Nobody ever really waits for death, except those who are truly ready. My grandma was going into the hospital for major surgery, and her doctor had said that there was a fifty-fifty chance that she might not survive it. I don't know how ordinary people from regular families deal with this kind of news. But for my out of the ordinary family with its absolutely nontraditional upbringing, morals, and values, and its dysfunctional ways, this meant utter chaos.

As *free* and *spontaneous* as my grandma had lived her life, her children had grown up giving new meaning to these words. You could say that Earline Griffin had led a secular lifestyle without many boundaries, and that's how she allowed her kids to come up after her. She was one of six children herself, five sisters and one brother. They were raised on a small farm off the Wakefield Road in Courtland,

Virginia, by parents who were a cross between the secular world and the church. Henry and Margaret Greene, better known as Bogey and Tanka Greene, were good, hardworking people. While Grandma Tanka was prone to serving the Lord and being in church every Sunday, Granddaddy Bogey did it *not so much*. In fact, he was prone to break out into a cussing fit in whatever requests or conversations he made. Rumor has it that Bogey Greene didn't take any shit from nobody, and he never had any trouble with the white folks around town. He worked his farm, but he didn't take any shit from nobody, and neither did his six children. That's the way he brought them up, but rest assured, it was *in their blood*. One thing the Greene's could and would do was raise hell. It started with my grandma and her siblings. If you messed with one of them, you had to fight them all.

My grandma was the fourth daughter and the fifth child. She and her siblings were something else back then and even through adulthood. The four girls were attractive women who loved money and men who could provide it. It wasn't so much about how the money was made but more about how the money was spent. The Greene women had a history of hooking up with big spenders. The more dangerous or risky the man, the more interested they were. They were not afraid to take risks, and they took risks with their men, their money, and even their lives.

My grandma lived at the top of her game and had the time of her life. She worked a government job at the Naval Supply Center in Norfolk where she made more money than women her age in our area. She was smart, bright, and had good business sense. She learned how to make money and how to hustle. But the flipside of it all was that my grandma not only had a keen sense for business; she had a keen sense for living life on the edge. She was a risk taker.

At one point, my grandma had purchased two vans and was

carrying two full loads of employees from the Franklin, Southampton County, and surrounding areas to the Portsmouth and Norfolk Naval Shipyards every day for years. She knew how to make a dollar. She loved people and people loved her because she always seemed to have money. Whatever the latest style was, my grandma wore it. Whatever the newest vehicle was, my grandma had it. The best furniture, she had it; and the most expensive foods, she ate them. She was the woman that all of her friends longed to be, and she knew how to make everybody around her feel special. She loved to splurge.

Earline Griffin was a hustler, and not only did a zero tolerance for bullshit run through her veins, she was a gambler at heart. Her risk taking did not begin or end with the men in her life. She was a risk taker who played numbers and popped cards—sometimes all night long. She was a bona fide card shark, and for all of her life she had been the luckiest woman I'd ever known. I don't know how many numbers she hit for large sums of money. I don't know how often she was the recipient of some minor, unfortunate event that resulted in a lawsuit and mega payments. She even managed to hurt her back on her government job, was paid large sums in lump sums, and was set for the rest of her life. All of her friends were card players like her. She hosted many card games at her house on weekends. There would be food, drinks, fried fish, and chicken.

My grandma was a woman you didn't want to cross. She was a beautiful woman with a beautiful, giving heart. But she had her limits. Most of her friends were men and *good-looking* men. Though she'd had some men in her life, she met and married my Granddaddy Jake, a nice, easy-going man. More importantly, he had a steady job at the local meat packing company, and he loved my grandma so much that he believed in giving her every dime he had *if she asked for it.* She made more money than him, but Jake won her heart because he worked to give her the world, and he let her do exactly what she wanted. In addition, because he worked at the meat packing company, my grandma never had to buy meat from the grocery store. That was life on the flipside with Earline Griffin. My Grandma had to be in control, and if she was not, she could be cold, calculating even. It was in her blood. Greene women have to be in charge of our own destinies. So Jake was a jewel. He didn't mind my grandma playing cards, playing her numbers, or hanging out all night long so long as she came back home to him. When they were happy, which seemed like all of the time, we were happy, because they were the kind of folks who would just spoil you to death.

My grandma loved money, made money, and didn't mind spending money. She leaves a legacy of living well and enjoying life, and it was passed on to everybody in the bloodline apparently. But the problem is that most of the bloodline forgot the work ethic part. Whether they were her kids, her nieces and nephews, or random children in the neighborhood, if you were in her presence, you were somehow blessed. Her children and most of her grandchildren had happy childhoods. They rarely went lacking. Every one of my grandmother's children had cars to drive when they were teenagers. My mother even had a credit card at sixteen in the sixties. I don't know many Black kids her age who did. If you wanted freedom, you had it in Earline Griffin's house, but if you didn't know how to handle it, it may have been the beginning of your end.

My grandma was no expert parent or even a model for one, but she believed in being a good provider. She wasn't into enforcing a whole lot of rules, and her children loved it. She didn't run a tight ship. She spent money on her children, feeding them, dressing them, spoiling them, getting them good jobs, and keeping them out of trouble. She believed in family and friendship. If you were my grandma's friend, you too, were the recipient of everything she had. There was nothing that she wouldn't do for you. Once you were in her inner circle, she treated you like family.

Being the shark she was, there were always people around and always people in the house, which is one of the reasons that I was not allowed to even be around after dark on most weekends. It was a constant party *down the road*. I lived with my other grandmother, and she limited the time I could spend there. But Grandma Earline's house was always the place to be. She lived just two houses down, and for the first half of my life, getting up each day and going *down the road* to her house was the absolute highlight of my day. My mother's siblings were not much older than me, and you could bet your last dollar that there was always a good time to be had in that house.

My grandma and her husband worked all of the time, and so her teenaged kids were often home alone. When my grandma got home from work, she just seemed to glow, never upset about how she found her house. She often came bearing gifts, lavish dinners, or with the idea that she would load us all up and take us out to dinner. On weekends, sometimes she'd even take us all out for breakfast and lunch. Her kindness and free spirit knew no end and had no boundaries. If you were there when she was in the blessing business, you got blessed. Like God, she was not a respecter of persons. She didn't believe in that. My grandma was not a deeply religious woman or even a churchgoer, but she surely knew how to love and treat her neighbors.

She was a light drinker but most seriously a smoker, and later in life an abdominal aortic aneurism would make her quit smoking cold turkey. I remembered riding with her in her brand new Cadillac with the windows down and the smoke being caught up in the breeze. She was a beautiful woman, and sometimes I used to just love to watch her hold a cigarette in her hand. She did it with such class. But eventually, she would completely put down the cancer sticks. As these things go, she had developed this aneurism and was told to allow doctors to keep close watch on it because if it grew and exceeded a certain size, it could pop, and she'd be dead in an instant.

The next decade would be filled with non-smoking days and more grandkids and great-grandkids to come. My grandmother was getting older, but you'd better not tell her that. She was young at heart, and she still loved a good time. Crowds of people continued to congregate at her house, wherever that was, because she moved a lot. Her house was always a hangout. She was not the biggest card shark anymore, and Granddaddy Jake had gone home to be with the Lord, but she still enjoyed her friends and a good card game every now and again. Age often catches up with you when you least expect it, but my grandmother had made a vow to enjoy every single moment of her life. She never had regrets. That's the kind of woman she was. She made decisions, but she was always grown enough to live with the consequences. Earline Griffin never dwelled on past mishaps. Even at this late stage in the game, her mind was still on her money, and money was always on her mind. But this time, there were a whole lot of mouths to feed.

My grandma had not only been a benevolent mother to her own children, but her generosity spilled over into the next generations of grandkids and great-grandkids whom she loved and spoiled. She loved her grandchildren, sometimes to a fault. She would spend money on lawyers, rehab, light bills, overdue rent, and whatever debts her children, grandchildren, and friends owed. She would give you the shirt off her back, and she often did. Once you establish this kind of trend, it's hard to break. Every generation became a little less responsible, a little less ambitious. This kept my grandma constantly tossing up bills and paying for the mistakes of others. She stayed behind and in debt, *robbing Peter to pay Paul,* so to speak . . . all at the expense of her family and friends.

So the day came when the aneurism reached its feared size, and my grandma needed surgery. Doctors told her that it was a big risk, the surgery, and that she might not survive. It was a fifty-fifty chance; she could live or die. I can imagine that she, being the gambler she was, weighed the possibilities. On the one hand, she could survive and have a few more years with her family that seemed to be less and less sane by the day. I guess there really is a method to madness. She could visit and interact with her grandkids and continue to help out financially as she had been doing for the last few years. On the other hand, if she didn't wake up . . . she would be *at peace.* She may not have known what kind of peace, but she would have peace and, for sure, freedom.

So the day came, and because I was out of the country, my mom kept me in the loop via text message. I had been in South Korea for a year, but I talked with my grandma every month, sometimes a few times a month. I could hear it in her voice. She was changing. She wasn't the strong woman I had known my whole life. Her body was frail before I left, and I knew that her time would come, that she would one day leave me. Even her voice over the phone was not as strong as it used to be. On the day of her surgery, she went into the hospital early in the morning because she needed a last minute blood transfusion.

I received my first text that she was going into surgery and that it would be an eight-hour procedure. Midway through the surgery, I received another text that all was well. I had been praying, and I even had my Facebook friends praying with me. At the end of the surgery, I received another text saying that all was still well, the surgery was a success, and they were waiting to see her in recovery, in the ICU. She had not come around, but doctors believed that everything was still going to be okay. It was late into the night, and my family members went to my uncle's house nearby; they planned to return early in the morning to check on her. Some time in the wee hours of the night, *something went wrong.* I began to get emergency texts that there was a blood clot and the need for another emergency surgery. "Call ASAP" is what all of the messages said. When I finally did get to my phone and dial all of the numbers that I had to dial internationally, the voice on the other end stopped me dead in my tracks. It was my mother, and she was crying and wailing in a way that I had never heard her cry before. All I could make out was "She's not going to make it!" There was uncontrollable sobbing. Because my nerves were not prepared to deal with mourning or this sad news, I had to hang up the telephone.

As a person of faith, I prayed. I believed God, but I wasn't so sure what I had believed him for. I had watched my grandma live a wonderful life and establish a legacy of helping others and giving to those in need all around her. I had watched her rise to the top, and I had witnessed her also sink to the very bottom in her constant efforts to bail out family members and friends in trouble . . . all because she loved too much. Her life had become a pitiful existence, and most of us knew it. We had grown tired and angry sitting idly by watching family members, neighbors, and friends take advantage of her kindness. I had grown angry with family members who had come to abuse her physically and financially. My grandma was a risk taker. She was a gambler. She had risked her life for people who didn't seem to appreciate her, some of them, the way a matriarch needed to be appreciated. Her grandchildren, many of them, took her for granted and failed to give her the respect that she deserved. This was disheartening to me because this strong tower of a woman who had given her all in life for everyone else had been reduced so much by the same people she broke her back to care for every day of her life. And so, with the news that she was not going to make it, I was surprisingly *at peace* that she would finally have *some peace.*

It was the day that nobody had awaited, but after crying at the thought of never seeing her again, I smiled and knew that she was finally free, free to be the spontaneous spirit that she was born to be. She was destined to rise. But near the end of her life, she didn't do anything of the sort. They clipped her wings and kept her down. I watched her become someone I'd never imagined, and finally, I was content with the fact that she was released, even in death, to be the beautiful woman she had been born to be.

Until the end, my grandma made her final decision just as she had made most decisions all of her life, as a *risk taker*. She exerted full control and took *one last risk*, the risk of not waking up to what she had created, nurtured, loved, and perhaps lost. If you ask me, *she had won*. Earline Griffin had hit her final number. She had won her largest jackpot, for to be absent from her Earthly body was to be in the eternal presence of something greater. The time had come. What her children, grandchildren, family, friends, and even her foes finally had to do was pay her what they owed her.

Misfit Island

Mardra Sikora

I arrived at the front drive in shoes worn thin while the sun broke over the horizon. The haunted darkness of the red brick building didn't brighten with the sunlight.

Well, here it is. Although I knew all along it wasn't a literal island, I sat on the curb's edge and stared up at the bleak windows without any coverings, every corner sharp and unforgiving and wished it looked . . . safer. *What did you expect? A great castle with iron gates?* No signs advertised what went on in this building, no banner full of hope for those in need. Like me.

My journey to *the Island* began with a note to find John Smith, my first contact in the network. Each new contact led me from point to point, house to house, until four months later I found myself at the outer gate. The folks in the network told an old tale with hope for a real-life happy ending, the children's story "The Island of Misfit Toys," a place for toys just wrong enough that they were discarded as useless, unfit, and left on a lonely isle. Until one day their benevolent leader, presumably the guy who stuck them there in the first place, rescued them from exile and took them to loving homes.

Everyone wanted home to be where differences are forgiven,

maybe even celebrated. *Everyone in the network, that is.*

A truck drove up the right hand side of the drive and rumbled to a stop just out of my line of vision. I moved toward it to see the man roll open the back full of boxes. He grabbed several and went into the building. *I'll take one in and look around. If I don't like it, I'll leave. They'll never know I was here. Brilliant.* After testing a few top boxes, I found one with a safe weight and made my way through the side door.

The interior corridor loomed still and antiseptic. *Hmm. Maybe just offices on the first floor or a cover of some kind.* I spotted an elevator and entered. *One floor at a time,* I told myself as the doors closed me in.

When they opened on floor two, the commotion grabbed and shook me far worse than a Grimm's fairy tale. Young and old wandered semi-corralled in varied states of awareness. I wandered into the large room with yellowed walls and small gate-like partitions that kept the occupants in small groups. One young woman screamed from her wheelchair, her arms flailing to an unknown rhythm. The scream didn't sound of pain, only a hollow yell that proclaimed, "I am here!" Another woman, older and graying, walked past me mumbling a string of profanities. "Goddamn-shit-bitch," she said to herself. Others whispered and babbled, each looked not at each other but to the air ahead. I didn't recognize anything articulate enough to resemble a request. I watched the individuals melt together into a cloud of mere existence. If I smelled fear, it was surely my own as I stopped, fixated. My fingers dug into the box, clutching it like a shield.

One clear voice cut through the clutter. "What are you staring at?" A young man came toward me. "What do you want?"

"What?" I shook myself back into the moment. "Oh. I . . . I'm . . . " *The box, stupid.* "I'm delivering this."

"What is it?"

"What is it?" I repeated numbly.

Making sounds of exasperation, he pulled the top of the box open and said, "These things go to medical." I didn't move. "Third Floor. Third Floor!" And he marched back into the commotion. "Alright, kids," I heard as I turned and entered the elevator, "Who's up for music time?"

I leaned against the back wall of the elevator; my limbs trembled. Two weeks since I last slept in a safe-house bed instead of on a bench or a floor while I traveled north. My stomach rolled. "I know, I'm hungry too," I said. *Keep it together.* The burning from my stomach's center traveled through my blood to every nerve in me. *Is this the destiny I've chosen for us? Is this my child's future?*

The doors opened to the dimly-lit halls of floor three. There were rooms along the passageway, tunneling the sunlight through doorways. I stepped out and appraised this floor, *medical he called it,* was probably the same layout since the hospital's original design, rooms along each side of the corridor and a mid-area nurse's station. Only muffled sounds came from the rooms.

A woman and boy walked down the hall; he struggled with effort and the woman guided him one step in front of the next. When the child collapsed, the woman saw me and called out—"Come here!"

I dropped the box and rushed to the pair. The boy came in and out of his seizure. The woman and I turned him on his side, and she instructed me to rub his legs. She spoke melodically, rubbed his back and arms and we waited for the spasms to work their way from him. The woman, nearly as small as a child herself, looked old enough to be my grandmother, at least.

"Can you carry the boy to his room?" she asked.

"Uh, no," I said. "I don't think I can."

"Hm," she said.

"I'm pregnant." I blurted out, feeling the need to justify myself.

"How?" she asked.

How?

"How far along?"

"Oh." I blushed. "Six months."

"Oh dear, you need to get to the fifth floor. That's where you want to be." Her smile comforted me. The boy's breathing smoothed while we hovered over him. "Go across the hall there to room 12. Tell Alena I need her. Then off with you. Fifth floor."

Again, I followed the instructions that led me back to the elevator. *Okay. Deep breath. It's going to be ok.* My cover was broken. *It's not like anyone else will help us. This is our only hope.* I pushed my trembling hands deep into my pockets as the elevator door opened. It didn't feel like hope.

The door opened to floor five. Various rug pieces covered the central open area with some spots worn through. Children's artwork colored the walls. A small group of toddlers clapped hands as they took turns rolling a ball between them. School-age children sat in a circle singing songs with an adult—*a teacher?* The room vibrated with energy and color. It felt alive.

Is this a mirage in this Misfit Island? Can there be laughter and song in our future? I took in a deep breath as I stepped forward trying to comprehend the scene, but my shaking limbs and exhaustion pushed me to the floor. Strangers rushed with surprised and kind voices and then . . . nothing.

My dream took me back to the day I received the blood test results.

"This is for the best," the doctor said. I stared at him in this dream as I had in 100 dreams since these words came from his lips: "Soon, this will all be behind you." My throat closed, denying any reply. The doctor coughed into his fist. "The nurse will make the arrangements."

"How's next Tuesday?" she asked. I shook my head. "Oh, a week from Thursday?" I shook my head. I wanted to run but felt weighted. I looked at her. My eyes pleaded for another option. "It's harder the longer you wait," she said.

"Harder?" I managed to whisper. *Is anything harder than giving my body over to have my own child killed within me?* I couldn't agree to a date. I couldn't . . .

She left the room and another, stern-looking nurse entered. "You understand," she spoke as she wrote on an appointment form, "it is against the law to bear a deformed child. You do not have the right to inflict this burden on our system." She handed me the slip of paper. It said *Contact John Smith at . . . the network will lead you to the Island.* She took my shoulder and whispered, "You must act quickly." She turned without expression and left me alone. I folded the paper and gripped it inside my jacket pocket.

That night I packed a backpack and our journey began.

In that small place between awake and asleep I heard a girl's voice. "Is she sick?"

"I don't know, Sarah, maybe she's just tired."

"Wow. That's really tired."

"Yes."

"She looks cold."

"Does she? Well, why don't you get her another cover?"

"Got it." Feet scampered away and returned. I felt the warmth of an added layer. I opened my eyes. "She's awake!" Sarah jumped with delight. She peered towards me, her slightly flattened eyes squinting. "You okay?"

I looked at my concerned helper, her round cheeks and youthful face. "Um, hmm," I said. "Thank you."

"Okay, Sarah." The woman waved her away. "You've been a very good nurse. Now go help Anthony." Then she walked towards me. "Do you know where you are?"

Maybe, I propped myself on the cot and took inventory of my surroundings. The large uncovered windows made the room cold and bright. Two other cots were within arm's reach. In the hall the noise of children and adults working and playing matched the sounds of the fifth floor before I collapsed. "Misfit Island," I said.

"Okay. Now tell me *why* you are here." Her face calm, the suspicion showed in her voice; it came as no surprise. A remodeled hospital full of illegal children and the adults that dared to care for them needed to be both secure and still provided for, a tightrope of opposing needs.

"I . . . I'm pregnant," I told her.

Her expression softened and she sat on the cot next to me.

"Six months," I said.

"You've come far?"

The tears kept under strict control mile after mile, now flowed. I ignored them and so did the woman.

"I suppose you're hungry then?" she asked. I nodded and attempted to wipe my cheeks nonchalantly. She brought bread and broth; the child in my mid-section rolled visibly around. "Oh my!" she said. "No one would believe you're carrying a baby but for that! You're so thin, that baby takes all the room you've got." I smiled, not really having another response. "Boy or girl?" she asked.

"Boy." Her eyes asked the next question. "Down syndrome," I answered.

She patted me on the shoulder. "Don't worry, girl, you made it. You'll both be safe here." Then she quickly turned out of the room.

I looked down and ignored the tears that fell into my soup.

Forging Freedom Volume 2

About Our Authors

Natasha Bennett is a Canadian author and has been previously published at Lyrical Press, Lilibridge Press, Fear and Trembling, and Static Movement. She also has an upcoming novel release at Belfire Press. In her spare time, she likes to watch horror movies and help other authors on the road to publishing. She lives with her husband and two cats.

Gillian Burdett is a freelance journalist and high school English teacher. She writes for Clarity Digital Group on health, education and public policy issues and is a regular contributor to CBS Local Media. She holds degrees in Cultural Studies with a focus in literature and is a M.Ed. in Secondary Education. Her creative writing seeks to examine the intersection of public policy and private lives. She lives with her family in New York's Adirondack Park.

Dominic Cheverton is a twenty-six year old graduate of English Literature and Creative Writing at Aberystwyth University in Wales, UK, and is soon to be entering into a postgraduate course in Creative Writing. He has had a passion for writing since he was very young. Though "Hana Yori Dango" with Freedom Forge Press is his first publication, he hopes to publish many works of length in various genres, several of which are already under construction. He is a keen student of all periods of history, knowledge, music and imagination, his personal fiction recipe.

Lindsay A. Chudzik received her MFA in Creative Writing from Virginia Commonwealth University. Lindsay's short stories and creative nonfiction have appeared or are forthcoming in *Dogwood*, *Ghost Town*, Haunted Waters Press, and *Map Literary*, among others. Currently, she is an Assistant Professor of Writing at Virginia Commonwealth University and she serves on the Board of Directors for James River Writers. In her free time, Lindsay writes about trending women's and political issues for Maxwell's Playbook and leads a creative writing workshop at OAR for ex-offenders living in Richmond, Virginia.

Latorial Faison is an American military spouse, a mother, poet, author, and educator born and raised in Southampton County, Virginia by grandparents. She attended the University of Virginia and studied English Literature. Faison also holds a Master's degree in English from Virginia Polytechnic Institute & State University. She is the author of six books: *Secrets of My Soul*, *Immaculate Perceptions*, the trilogy collection, *Twenty-eight Days of Poetry Celebrating Black History*, and *Kendall's Golf Lesson*. Faison's writing has been published in *Southern Women's Review*, *Chickenbones*, *Underwired Magazine*, *Red River Review*, *Blackberry Magazine*, and alongside Iyanla Vanzant, Dr. Cornel West, and Tavis Smiley in the NAACP Image award-winning book, *Keeping the Faith: Stories of Love, Courage, Healing, and Hope from Black America*. In addition, this military spouse has been published in

Stars and Stripes Korea, Okinawa, Guam, and Kanto. Faison has taught college English for fifteen years at various colleges and universities across the U.S. to include Coker College, Johnson C. Smith University, Robert Morris University, and Virginia State University. She is an Assistant English Professor at Sejong University in South Korea, where she currently lives with her husband and their three sons. Faison's official website is www.latorialfaison.com.

Melinda Friesen decided she needed a hobby to avoid irritating her children to death. In the spring of 2010, she started her first novel. At the sixty page mark, she abandoned that story and started another, but that story was a dead end, too. It wasn't until she started writing YA that her writing took off. By the end of the year, she'd finished her first three novels. Writing transformed from a hobby into a passion. With ideas that wouldn't make full novels, she began writing short stories as well. In 2012 her short story, "Murdering Elegance," won first runner-up in the Lawrence House Center for the Arts Short Story Contest, was shortlisted in the *Freefall Magazine* Prose and Poetry Contest, then published in *Freefall Magazine.* "The Haggard Man" won grand prize in the 2013 Central Canada Lit Fest Short Story Contest and was published in *Metro News.* Her first flash fiction piece, "Marriage Enrichment," was shortlisted in the 2014 Freefall Magazine Flash Fiction Contest. In addition to producing short stories, Melinda has written ten novels. Her YA Science Fiction piece, *Solar,* was shortlisted in the Writer's Village International Novel Award Spring 2014. Her novel, *Enslavement,* the first book in the One Bright Future series, launched in the fall of 2014 from Rebelight Publishing Inc. Melinda Friesen, a native Oregonian, lives in Winnipeg, Manitoba, Canada, with her husband and four children. She blogs at www.melindafriesen.com.

Ken Goldman is a former Philadelphia teacher of English and Film Studies, and he has taught courses on Horror and Science Fiction in Film & Literature. An affiliate member of the Horror Writers Association, Ken has homes on the Main Line in Pennsylvania and at the Jersey shore depending upon the track of the sun and his need for a tan. His stories appear in over 720 independent press publications in the U.S., Canada, the UK, and Australia, and over thirty of Ken's tales are due for publication in 2014. Since 1993, his stories have received seven honorable mentions in The Year's Best Fantasy & Horror. He has written four books: his books of short stories, *You Had Me at Arrgh!!* (Sam's Dot Publishers), *Donny Doesn't Live Here Anymore* (A/A Publishers), plus an e-book, *Star Crossed* (Vampires 2 Publications); and a novella, *Desiree* (Damnation Books). His novel, *Of a Feather,* was published by Horrific Tales Publications (UK) in January 2014. Ken feels he would be famous except for the fact nobody seems to know who he is. However, he looks forward to the day when he and Stephen King are called to the dais and someone asks, "Who is that guy standing next to Ken Goldman?"

Dixiane Hallaj spent eleven years in the Middle East as part of her husband's extended family, listening as they shared their language, their history, and much of the refugee experience with her. More recently, she visited refugee camps on the West Bank where she listened to the stories of many of the women. Her own experiences and these stories formed the basis of her award-winning doctoral dissertation *Caught by Culture and Conflict,* and the novels *Born a Refugee* and *Checkpoint Kalandia.* She currently resides in Purcellville, Virginia, with her husband of 53 years and their cat named Dog. Find more of her books and interests on her website: http://www.dixianehallaj.com.

A contributor to *Forging Freedom I*, **A.J. Kirby** is the author of the novels *Paint this Town Red*, *Bully* and *Sharkways*, and the non-fiction book *Fergie's Finest*. His short fiction has been published across the web, and in magazines, anthologies and literary journals, as well as in two collections: *The Art of Ventriloquism* and *Mix Tape*. He was one of 20 Leeds-based authors under 40 recently shortlisted for the LS13 competition and his novel *Paint this Town Red* was shortlisted for last year's The Guardian Not the Booker prize. He blogs at http://paintthistownred.wordpress.com.

Jason Lairamore is a writer of science fiction, fantasy, and horror who lives in Oklahoma with his beautiful wife and their three monstrously marvelous children. He is a published finalist of the 2012 *SQ Mag* annual contest. His work is both featured and forthcoming in Third Flatiron publications, *The Blue Shift* magazine, *Postscripts to Darkness, Carnage: After the End Vol. 2*, Kerlak Publishing, Emby Press, *Great Escapes, Mad Scientist Journal, Planetary Stories*, and *Pantheon* magazine, to name but a few. You can find out more about Jason at http://www.facebook.com/#!/jason.lairamore.

Gerri Leen lives in Northern Virginia and originally hails from Seattle. She has stories and poems published or accepted in such places as *Escape Pod, Weird Tales, Spellbound, Sword and Sorceress XXIII, Spinetinglers*, and *She Nailed a Stake Through His Head: Tales of Biblical Terror*. She is editing an anthology, *A Quiet Shelter There*, which will benefit homeless animals and is due out in 2015 from Hadley Rille Books. See more at http://www.gerrileen.com.

Jordan Legg is originally from Oshawa, Ontario, with a degree in English and Creative Writing from the University of Windsor. He's been published in *Nebula Rift*, *Strong Verse*, *Allegory* eZine, and *On The Premises*. When not writing he enjoys drawing, soccer, reading, cycling, and maintaining his beard. Follow him on Twitter @JordanLegg2.

Lyn McConchie lives in the North island of New Zealand, on her small farm where she breeds colored sheep and has free-range geese and hens—plus a piglet, and a steer named TANSTAAFL. Lyn began writing professionally in 1990, and since then she has seen 32 of her books published and over 270 short stories, appearances ranging over eight countries and in four languages (English, Polish, Russian, and Spanish, and yes, her work gets about.). Lyn shares her 19th century farmhouse with an Ocicat named Thunder and 7,479 books. (And no, she isn't about to run out of reading any time soon.) Lyn was crippled in an accident in 1977, retired—from running a Government District Office—on medical grounds in 1988, and has been writing ever since. In addition to writing books and short stories, she also writes reviews and opinion pieces, consumer articles for her local newspaper, and is sometimes a live-theatre critic for them as well. When recently asked if she was ever bored, she said that she might find ten minutes available for that around mid-2025. Lyn's blog and website may be found at www.lynmcconchie.com.

George G. Moore is an aspiring novelist living in northern Virginia. He has had a short story published in the first *Forging Freedom* anthology and a technical article published in *PC Techniques*. He is a member of Pennwriters, Loudoun County Writers' Group, and the Round Hill Writers' Group. In addition to creative writing, he pursues various interests like golfing and reading outside of his day job managing a group of software engineers. He blogs at GeorgesPen.blogspot.com.

English teacher by day, editor **Val Muller** is the author of the

Corgi Capers kidlit mystery series (www.CorgiCapers.com), inspired by the two corgis that keep her on schedule if she ever tries to sleep in. She has also penned a horror novel, *Faulkner's Apprentice*, and a young adult reboot of Nathaniel Hawthorne's famous work, entitled *The Scarred Letter*. Her YA violin-inspired supernatural novel, *The Man With the Crystal Ankh*, and her coming-of-age tale, *The Girl Who Flew Away*, are forthcoming. You can learn more about her short fiction and everything else at www.ValMuller.com.

David Murphy's latest novella *Bird of Prey* was published in the USA in 2011. A previous novella *Arkon Chronicles* appeared in paperback from Silver Lake Publishing (a small press) in 2003. His novel *Longevity City* was published in hardback by Five Star, and well received, in 2005. His award-winning short fiction has been published and translated worldwide, including two chapbooks and a short story collection brought out in 2004 (reissued 2013). His latest book, a fiction-memoir called *Walking on Ripples*, was published by Dublin's Liffey Press in late 2014. Visit his website at www.davidmurph.wordpress.com.

Robert J. Santa has been writing speculative fiction of all kinds for thirty years, with numerous short works published in magazines, anthologies, and online. He lives in Rhode Island, USA, with his beautiful wife and two equally beautiful daughters. Robert is the editor-in-chief of Ricasso Press.

Mardra Sikora is a freelance writer, marketing consultant, and blogger by day and a fiction writer by night, leaving less time for sleep than one would expect. She is published in a scattering of literary journals and pursuing a few more. You can find more of her writing and social networking connections at www.mardrasikora.com.

Linda Harris Sittig lives in Loudoun County, Virginia, with her husband, where the Blue Ridge Mountains are the first to greet the dawn. She is the author of *Cut From Strong Cloth*, the first in the historical fiction series Threads of Courage. In her spare time, she travels with her family and enjoys spending time with her grandchildren. Visit Linda's website at www.lindasittig. com, or email her at linda@lindasittig.com. Her monthly blog pays tribute to women of the past who led extraordinary lives but did not necessarily achieve lasting fame: www.strongwomeninhistory. wordpress.com. Find her on Twitter: @lhsittig. Her motto: Every woman deserves to have her story told.

www.ingramcontent.com/pod-product-compliance
Lightning Source LLC
Chambersburg PA
CBHW070818180626
46818CB00001B/313